I0671093

-Scenes From Nowhere-

Michael Mc Aloran

#1-...Often, often from afar. In and out of speech, that's how it appears, that's how it is, to fool the absence into thinking that there was ever anything. But there isn't anything, no, not like that, the other way around. All the same, over and until again, beginning again, ramparts levelled and then the recurrence of it. No reason to argue, if it remains untrue, there'll be nothing either way. It's spoken for, silenced again. Yet out of less, or, perhaps more, rattling in the wind, something whole becomes the fragment, the naught. Nothing less or more splendorous, so they say, but they've never seen, it's never been seen, as if it could be seen, waste and wanton. Collapse and never yet be done, beneath a pit of sky, fruitless hands and the lifeless breathing. Never having been in the first instance, it seems likely, but no, no use in trying to reduce it to that. Night's pastures, something taken away, given back, never reclaimed, what of it...

...I can see the streets from here, it hasn't been long, it won't matter, the streets long and seemingly everlasting, until. I'll just sit here, smoking, it might, I'll drink too, all the wine that god sends me. I'll not succumb, there's no place for it, yet there's not much else, in spite of things. The sun might rise, I'll still sit here, it's too plain to describe, other than four white walls and a bed, table, chair and bookshelf; I take my meals elsewhere. All of that, useless fettering, I sleep alone, I drink alone, I smoke alone, I'll just sit here. Wandering about...what. I hold my breath intermittently, seeing if I'll burst, I might burst a blood-vessel, but no. Perhaps a heart-attack might be easier to induce, it could happen, I'll look into it, I will, I always do. There, it's been noted, I'll mend this whipped canine yet, I won't regret it, there's nothing left, often. Whipped? A little extravagant, okay then. But no nothing broken of which I am aware, so I say, and I believe in nothing. I'll see it through, says the naught, say the vapours, the mists, I know that I am lying, I'll exist for nothing, yet already nothing is all that I am. I'll spill my guts, then, if that'll make me happy, I'll be as purposeless as that, I will...

...Ah, to leap tied at the neck out through my window in some gesture of violent disgust -ha! And the women, with their hands covering the eyes of their children as they stare on in disbelief. Ah piss, fragment, naught, caved in beauty of a face obliterated. Yet no, better to...what. I'll never be back, either way, at least I'm frank about it. Yes out of less, or perhaps more, nothing, nothing. I'll sit here, I'll dream of my own mercilessness, my own vulgar display, it will be night -it is forever night! I'll rant and rave, curse, but I won't be bitter. I'll be a Christ of my own design, that'll do. Ah there is nothing wrong with it, nothing right and everything, no, there is everything, to be done with it. Chewing up the broken glass and meat of the spill of the guts, pissing one's last breath in some deserted alleyway -enough! That'll be it, I'll not care, I'll still breathe, to a point or not at all, I won't know, I'll shit myself, I won't care, I'll laugh the laughter of the gallows. I'll be found, it won't matter to me, some poor knave will find me, it's noted, to get along, I'll go back, I'll...No...

...All of this nothing, these breaths, winds, this night and its ever-recurrence, the die are cast, the die are my own, better out of this than in. Shadowless, limp, stone cold and more beautiful than ever before, so they say, those that say things like that, I'll be a babe again, no, I'll still be nothing, without glamour. I'll be silent, the silence silenced, of more use than ever before, I'll have come and gone, in my own time, I'll seize the day, nothing to it. No answer to the when or why or the whatever, so help me. Someone else will dwell here, it will have meant nothing but to no-one, but to me. Speech or non-speech, here and yet, the sun erased, no pace in these rixt bones. Sudden now, alack, nothing lacking and yet nothing else, translucent, gathered. Dreams are for lesser men, it's been said, I have said it before, I have no place, I have no time, I feel nothing for the flowers of the grave, there's nothing left of me to mourn, I wouldn't mourn for me, I mourn enough, yet it is not the same. Ah the stale night, here again, drinking again, smoking again, smoke in the eyes, false tears, vague, vacant almost, the sky above, no prayers from me it's been settled, that was settled long before now. No, I won't make a holy show of myself, I'll just recount the hours, no I won't, that's wasted time, in the minute, yes, in a minute now I'll rise and sit back down again. There won't be anything else, but for the street, quiet as it is, it is always quiet, it lends to the absurdity, I'll not be moved, I say, there, that's the ticket. I'll move, I'll have to, to empty the old body, whistling as usual, there, I know it now, I'll go back and forth and there will be nothing much, I might as well stare at the four walls, or not, perhaps lay here in the dark, who knows, what matter. Yet there may be days yet, I laugh, I laugh because I am lying, there may be days yet, there will be none and nothing more of this charade, this parade of languishing sterility. No reason to go elsewhere, not like in the old days, I'm done for now, until I rise again, I won't rise, I won't live, how can I not?, I exist. All in all, I can't live, no not anymore, by breach or breath or design, I'll dream of it, a lesser man's curse, stay here I say, I'll break, I'll shatter, there will be bone in the mix, I'll...No no more, no more words, I will speak no more, there'll be nothing, there is nothing more, yet still they arise and then recede. Nothing in that, I make notes, I don't sleep, I don't awaken, there is weather as always and the streets, variable, quiet, yet variable...

...No human contact, it's the only way, I see it no other way, miserable wretches all, I'd spit as soon as be kind to one, bury the head in the sand, yet there would be no fear of it, I'd spit in the eye as soon as be kind, a nightmare, disastrous, I concede, I never do. There's been none of that, not since I did, not since it was done, it was ever thus, I lie. I'll laugh again, there'll be laughter and wretched bones. There'll be the laughter or tears, I can't think of whose, perhaps there'll be none, there'll be mud in the eyes yet, a spark, something, oh I never know, I can't go back, I can't stomach it, not the coming or the going, proof by extraction, shadow by default, as if, no, shadow my arse, I was never shadow, I was never a dreamer, head in a vault of eclectic colourings, snap snap, fingers snapping, hence in the long run there will be night, yet it won't be dark, it won't be light, there'll be enough of that, I don't know, if at all, I'll stay silent, yet there'll be no scattered silences, there'll be a time for that, if I look upon it, if I evade it, if I close the door one last final time, having the knowledge of the induced heart-attack in my skull, that'll be the ticket, I'll lay there in my cot and drink my wine and that will be it, I'll slide easily, I'll not be surrounded, not by any of them, I'll sleep, it will be done, there's nothing I can't do, I will. And the way of it, yes having been found, perhaps the reek of me will drift out under the door, yet I'll be clean, I'll wash my bag of bones, under the arms and the crotch and the arse, one can't be disrespectful, perhaps I'll buy a new suit, a fresh shirt, I'll wear a good tie, I will, yes that's it, I'll be dressed up for the fair, perhaps there might be sun, night even, I'm not particular, it won't matter anyhow, nothing matters anyhow, I haven't mattered yet, never will, not even in love's chambers where she used to dwell, long afar, long gone now, ghosts of catacombs long lost, dead indeed, never saw it either, I never knew, I'll never know....

...Ah spit, nothing there either, a vague trace, a vague trace of the winds of feeling, I'll drink my wine, it will be sublime, no, that serves only to carry me on, I'll spill my wine down the sink, I'll open another bottle, I'll drink from that, straight down into the gullet, I'll sit in my chair at my table, I'll listen for something, the voices voiceless, echoing spasms of subtle speech, non-speech, non-time, there will be a time, so I say, not likely. I'll empty out my head, I'll take a shovel to it, a grave, I'll dig a grave, aggrandized, no flies on me though, I'll dig a grave of silences, worms in the skull, I'll listen for them, as if they could be heard or spoken of, their whisperings, their silences. Hands dead and nothing less will suffice, never having begun, never having followed, counter-speech. That's the way, it still beats, I don't want it to beat yet it still beats, what now, at the beginning never having ended, so I say, so the echoes say, I can't count them. Broken by stillness in a death dream of accord, of sun, of having to go on, of night endless, figuratively, nonsense all off it, the slate wiped clear and yet never knowing of it, dare I say, I taste the words on my tongue, lies, all of it, caring for nothing, feeling less and less....

...Well to be come undone, lapsing to and fro, stillness of the frost settling, I remember the field where we lay, the soil was ploughed, frozen, we lay there anyhow and watched the clear night sky, I in she, no way back now, no not ever. No, no time for the tears welling in the eyes, for the flesh abandoned, this is of another time. I'll not sleep tonight, I'll just sit here with my wine, listen to the echoes, watching the vapours, a fool, no I don't regret. All of this and still to become undone again, I'll swing yet, yet I thought it was all settled, I'll sleep it off, there, it's decided, I'll let it all slide, I'll have forgotten in the morning, I'll start again, I won't, I'll have the choice, it won't matter a damn either way, I'll still burn, what's left of me, and no other way about it and no way to get on with it, seeing no way, a curse, following through, beating on the walls, this or that, a flimsy response, not like the noose, I'll shut up now, I'll cease, no-one is listening anyhow, nothing changing from the day to day, the night to night, just the breath, fluctuating needs. I haven't eaten today, I don't care for it, perhaps I'll starve myself, no, too much time, a horrible business. Yet the embers of she, that's not what this is about, yet the embers of she, no, I can't go back, worse things have happened, I'm silenced, teeth in the grass from a broken jaw, lapsing again, falling silent, head to toe in nothingness, it will never again be said, I love you, I never did, I thought I did, she loved me and I, and now...

...Ah what the sun could give me back if it shone, deeply in this, taking me back this night, no, a windbag, I'll talk out of my arse until the sheep are sheared, ah yes, the old days, I hated it, I hated them, those were the times of dread, I should have taken the shears to him, I'd have done time for him, the bastard, I should have, I should have gotten away sooner, but no, not a penny to my name, where could I have gone, what else would have become of me, but this nothing. Ah spare the child and bless the rod, look at the cut of me, I'm practically dead, yes I'll take another one, there, that's the ticket, the price of it, I'll be gathered up for nothing, gathered bones of nothing. And but for the sod turned there'll be no extra effort, the poor sod won't know, he'll just do his job, digging away, till it's over with, much like myself, just fading away, it was never there to be lost, it never had, there never was, no meaning, no, not love, no, nor the chandelier heart, the extras, her legs spread, the pale ashen flesh of her, the drapery of her red hair and the caress of her voice, and such words, no, I'm never going back there again, it's finalized, I'll be, no not of her, I've had enough, no nothing, lapsed again, in the dregs, in the silence of it, listening to my breath, I'll not scream, I'll take it gracefully, there'll be nothing, that's all I'll be, all there is or is not, they never knew for sure, I'll never know, it has come to this, so be it...

#2-...Let it...Let it be damned...What with the foraging, the absence and the drain, the piss of this and that. Succumb I may, drought could be said of it, dry sands, here in the sun, a day, some night, there'll be no sleep anyhow. There hasn't been, not for a long time, I'll rest yet, I will, it'll be like old times never known, with a rattle and a yolk, a bustle and a fro. Some sense knocked into me, so it was said. Ah, begin again, I didn't intend to, the dam is broken. It'll never seal, there'll be something taken from me yet, I've nothing left, nothing left to give away, awry with breath counting down the beats of the pulse. Into what, some way or other, it'll never do, there'll never be enough, there was never enough, up to the gills in flesh and bone. That's how it stands, it says so, I'll never know, I'm both prisoner and jailor, waiting in the station, the eyes half-dead and the sky full of nothing much, a few stray gulls, a stream of white, blood on my handkerchief, it's all wrong but it was never otherwise. No, I'll not bother, let it be damned but for today, a long day, head in a vice of cold colours, screaming without sound, without echo, without purpose, I'll go yet. I'll pick the dying flowers, I'll eat them as I go, there'll be no shadows, it'll keep, I'll walk and there'll be nothing, there'll be death in my eyes, sun or night or not it won't matter, I can live with that, I can die of that, no, not today, I'll continue, there'll be a dance in the flames yet. Not a speech, not a sound, not a voice, no, not for today, it's noted. I'll flourish, I'll listen to the small talk, listen to the women, watch the women, watch them all, in my secrecy, behind my dark glasses, cane at my side as always as if I were a blind man, they won't know, and me with the half-rod and them jiggling and bouncing around in their rawness. Ah, the sun, I'll never lose my wings of it. I'll smoke, yes, that's the ticket, perhaps. A head full of molten rocks and I'll smoke, it'll come again, I'm never prepared, it runs all over me like serpents ablaze, leaving no traces, I'll counter yet or I won't, it won't matter, it doesn't matter, the sky is darkening, I'm alone...

...Ah yes, here again, the walls again, the drought following me, the drought follows, septic, almost darkness now. A candle lit and my wine, rough this morning, hence the sea air, it never does any good, I almost vomited. And the tap-tap-tapping away of the cane, I almost smiled, an old lecher, well there's a laugh, yes, it's true. Nothing, still as ever present, yesterday's echoes, the echoes of the noose's shadow, hardly perplexed enough today to, I won't count on it. One of my turns, I am forever turning, forever at it, I'll never again recount, so I say of it. And yes, not much, there'll be manys a silence tonight, manys a folding of ashen cloth, manys a storing away of clothes no longer of any use to anyone, except perhaps given away, some use in death then, I never thought, what of it. I see myself stretched out, pasty faced, skin like wax, hair combed, fingernails clipped, the nicotine stains removed from the fingers. What am I waiting for, I don't know, as if I were afraid, yet I'm not afraid, it seems as pointless as the next thing. Not a flame left but the candle, none in me, to a dying man I would not sell this life, he'd be better off without it. All for one and one for all my arse, there, it's noted, not much use in that either. I'll have some more wine, drink up my quota, it's never enough, though it sends me away, never unto sleep, the candle extinguished, no more the frenzies or the pangs, lying here alone in the stillness, listening to vague sounds of the traffic from outside coming in, through the crack in the window, the coming and the going, forever in transit, nothing else to be doing, in transit here or there again, folly all...

...I think I may, here it comes again, the old card, a fresh face upon it, I have no time, it's wasted on it, the old card and here it comes, orchestra of the failing pulse, the failing skull. Yes -take it back!, I'd never go back, not now, not a hope, for what good reason, glad to be done with it, it's been said, it's been noted, through again, all said and all done. Strange the light tonight, a balm, I'm cold, I lie here shivering, I'm warm but I'm cold, ice in the veins, nothing new, not in this condition. I'll see it through, no, I'll hardly live, I'll be erased, it won't matter a damn. There'll be nothing, I'll take my meals, I'll smoke afterwards, I'll drink my wine, perhaps elated for a moment or two, that's it, I'll be a little drunk, I'll put on a little show of graciousness, they'll help me out of my chair, I'll leave them my customary tip, I'll be alone. I'd gladly spit in their eyes, I'll put on a little show for them, the waitresses will giggle as always, that will be all. I'll walk home in the evening light to my room, the key will be turned, into the room and to done with them all again. Back to this, back to nothing, out of nothing, nothing out there, a little more wine, a smoke or two, and here I am, where I began. Back again, in the filth of it, in the meat of it, in the silence of it, holding my breath again in case I might...burst. Though not much use to linger on that, or very much else for that matter, I'll be grateful, but I won't know of it. Pains in the chest elect the same thoughts every time -Yes!, a heart-attack, it's over with! Oh what a wretched bastard I am, oh how I loved, once in a while, springing back into misery and despair. The room is fading, it'll soon extinguish, I mean the candle, knowing my luck there'll be no surcease for me, no not until the very end of it, I know it, they're keeping me alive just to torture me, no, that's preposterous, I never believed that once, no not until the end of it, I know it, I know nothing...

...Heave away/ heave ho, yes of course, like a revolving door of mirrors, snared teeth illumined in the dark, but no it's just the sun through the blinds, alive again, as if I had gone somewhere, not much chance of that. Up now and wash and pare that lugubrious gait of yours, I say to myself, I'll stay intact, it has to be done, it's nothing, what utter shit. Sick from wine once more, where are my manners, I'll smoke first, I'll piss, I'll empty my bowels, how many times, how many ways, what a design this is. Forever with the seize the day, as they say, as if it were a liberty, no not from the start, I should have done it years ago, there would have been none of this, though it matters little, either way, but I would have been done with this, I would have never known, and I'd have known better than this, I'd have known less of nothing, perhaps, in my own way, ah I am talking out of my arse. And so the blade again, in the mirror again, lathering, spitting out the morning blood, clearing the lungs, not a bit of decorum once alone. The blade paring away at the face, always wondering of the wrists, no not deep enough that time, strange the scar tissue, luckily the tendons were un-severed. That wouldn't have been anything worth shouting about, hands with fingers unable to move, nothing noted then. And the blood. No no more the rage, no, not as if I bled it out of me, as if it could be done with, as if it could be done, a failure, all in all, I failed. I stare into the mirror, straight into the eyes, nothing, still here and still ablaze, salve of no purpose, cold, no regret, nothing else to be said of it, as if words were worthy, no, not a sound, not in the light of day...

...This old hulk of bone and meat, this rind, I cease to look, I can't, I look away. Ask of me something, I ask myself, I'll know the answer, it'll not stay concrete, it won't, I'm telling you. I laugh, I bite my fist, there might be tears, I'll find out, ever unto. Nothing today, not yet, nothing worth noting, perhaps I'm asleep, perhaps I'm dreaming, but no. Ah getting to thinking of it is of no use, though better at night, always, close to dreaming, sleepless, rot, I'll have to leave. The day in hand, out of my depth, what is my depth, what do they mean. I'll dress myself up as if fit for a wedding or a funeral, no reason, just in case. No chance of that, I can't decide if I care or not, I will, I'll go on with it, without purpose, that will be my purpose, I'll lie to myself in order to be, I'll do it again, with much fervour, I can't, I can't and I won't. The dead of my life circle me, a circle of vapours from out of which their forms appear, but nothing more, done now, vacant again. Ah to hell with it I'll just sit here bollock naked in front of my window, with the blinds drawn halfway. The sun on my balls, yes, I'll drink some wine, nothing else, nothing else, I'm not walking the promenade today. Death and sleep and the in-betweens. Silences echoings of dreamed speech, drifting through, as if they were taking something's place. Ah what an endeavour, what a shit-stained lie, I'm breathless, another drink, yes, I'll not care. There's not much left they can do to me now, the bastards, whoever they might be, or very much left to my own devices, as I am, cleaving away, I'll never last...

#3-...Not a step...Not a glance...Not a word...No, not today, though I might forget altogether. I might be overcome, yet, who's to know, in what fashion, I'll not resign myself, no. Perhaps I'll speak louder, I'll not murmur, I'll not stammer, even in an empty room, no, it won't do. All lies, all for nothing, I've said it before, in case it's forgotten, no, I won't forget that either. Not with the meandering, the clogged tongue turning in the ashen mind, there'll be a death, somewhere, it'll matter it won't matter. Ah the dead sun, the sun alive, sometimes, clamour, silence, the rot and the shining of it. Pick a card, any card, the lungs of it, the eyes subdued. Time does not pass, I've no sense of it, there's nothing to it, I laugh to myself, I'll laugh myself to death, some might disagree. Ah well at least there are these walls, they may be the death of me yet, manys a four walls have killed a man. The silence of it, this non-space, I'm conditioned to it, I don't see how it was ever to work. Solace or the grappling fingers, manys a punch dealt in anger, nails clawing at the emptiness, tears in a dead absence. Never enough nothing, nothing erased, nothing claimed, nothing added, nothing taken away. Ah spit, this is vile, it'll never do, this carousel of night, kaleidoscopic death. They come and go, as if they had never been, some of them are no more, it's been noted, it's been said. They come and go and so much the better when they are gone, no more the shadow, the in-dreaming of it, the false light, the bitter spit, the claws to the guts, no, better off, I'll dig my own. Well to hell with it, it's no use, impossible, we can't, we're better off, waste upon waste ground, I know better. No sense in settling settling, no sense in turning either, lapsing into dead space, drowning in gardenias...

...Hope lest it be abandoned, that's what I say, yes, without it, nothing, there's no trick of the light, no martyrdom of having been sold the lie. Ah hope, grandest of illusions, only the snared animals know of it, not knowing the lie, praying as they burn, yes, what of it. Hoping on and off, for the end, they know, hoping to survive, as if. All that will be known in the end is the certainty, of there being none, of having been elected to this, thrown into waste, birthed into death as the blood streaks the sky, so they say, it's noted, spasm and desire and the Shadow. Not a whisper, I'll come undone yet, there'll be nowhere, I am, I am nowhere. Speaking or not speaking, it'll hardly be the death of me, yet it'll hardly show, doubtful. No, there'll be nothing known today, I can vouch for that, as much as any other day or night, I'll lie here, prostrated, anguished, I'll grind my teeth, the sun, the black sky, unto naught, from nowhere, a picture-postcard of perfect nothingness, the heart still pounding, blood of course, well said, I think. There'll be no dreams, I won't succumb, that's preposterous, I never sleep, it's been said. All the while all of this coursing, this ebbing and flowing around me, unto some kind of nowhere else, to be. I want no part of it, quite obviously, better off, etc....

...There are many paths, damnation is an open road, room for all and all for none, there, noted. Given that the road is open, I'll just lay there, in the middle, I'll wait, just like some of the rest, nothing better, nothing worth doing, barely audible, I'll whistle some tune or other, to keep the rats from out of my skull. There might be a bottle, some surcease, no I'd bring one, I'd owe them nothing, vile bastards, Get your own!, I'd say, I'd laugh. Ah yes, what a bloody circus, away in the head again, rambling, it must be the cold, I'm sick in the head I think, who can tell. No, I'll have to, the noose swinging me out of the window was the best yet, I'll daydream a while, perhaps, better yet to come. No no it won't do either, I'll have to get to the chair, I'll put my pants back on, fix my shirt, light a cigarette, I'll pour a glass. Nothing to eat today either, I'm not bothered, no, couldn't stomach it, I'll stay put. Still this going on business is so bloody tiresome, simply waiting, caught between one night and the next, colourless. I can't explain my staying, it's not in my temperament, to do such a thing, it's not as if I'm old, no. Still, nothing to show for it, shite and onions, what's it worth, you'll never know. A dead secret, just lying there, not even feeling the comfort of the casket, the absence of breath, you can't even breathe in your own stench, what an empty joke. Back-handed and yes, the benign laughter, echoing dementia of a sky tearing apart, yes it goes on, so will this, what. Ah the piss of it, it's raining, sometimes, often...I'll watch, I'll fool myself that I am observing. Only a quick shower, no, not yet, liven things up a little with the fresh smell of rain-soaked concrete coming in through the gap in the window, unlike piss, I know. Well we'll have another, I will, I'll have another too, that makes the three of us, ha! We'll toast a dead world, I'll laugh, I'll laugh too, the three of us all together, then...

...Ah night, useless stone...Echo of nothing left and the hard speech of useless fettering, lines erased, I'll say the poor queuing for bread, I'll put a little drama to it, there'll be none. Bang bang you're dead, ah the old sounds, wordless drama of breathing, taking it all in, the headlights search the walls yet there is nothing here, or perhaps my shadow, raised up on the bed like a madman, bottle in hand. Ask of the hatchet, ask of it, ask again, I'll follow on from naught. None, no I won't ask, ask who, who goes there, I am alone yet who goes there, half-light and a debased skeleton, pants open, halfway down the legs, no reason, oh reason, yes I was going to relieve myself, no not like that. What I intended to do was merely bounce on the bed a bit, I thought better of it, it might break, that wouldn't do. Like a child. I can't tell if I was a child or not, I scarcely was, as I recall. I remember the fields, we used to set them alight when the grass was fresh-cut in the sun, run like fuck, no-one coming, ever. And then it was back to that madhouse with the landmines and the egg-shells forever scattered. There was always something, it...no. The old powder-keg, I should have cut his throat like I intended to, disappeared, I recall I was seven, maybe eight. Ah sure he was beyond the pale. Better left alone, no life in that. Here and now. The here and now. A fierce brute of a man, dead now, might as well be, I don't bother with that business. Rarely. Ah the exile, Jesus, I'll spit and rant and curse every bastard, it's all there is, I'll never toss a coin, I did once, I lost,, the door closed, nothing doing, ever done. Unable to cease yet not willing, back to that old broken gramophone, Give up or give out, in whatever order pleases you. Settle now, no use in spilling your teeth, the ennui has killed manys a man, it's brutal. The abattoir lies everywhere, in every mind and in every body, yet it does not 'exist', it's been noted, guillotine laughter, headless once and for all. Abattoir indeed, fleshed petals and the flailing animals hanging from their chains, the throats slashed, kicking their last as the blood spills into the gullies. Christs every one of them. No better here, thinking that we think, dying over and over in a day, a night, nothing blessed, everything cursed, silenced, done in again. All for the in-between, the times of slate grey peace. Settle now, no use in spilling your teeth, there'll be other times, I'll take what I have, I'll take nothing, nothing again, I'll just sit here, I'll just sit here again...How and now head with the sorry echo, I say to myself, tap tap tapping at the chamber door...

#4-...Ah yes, better late than severed, alone, never knowing, knowing the undone it causes. Left suddenly behind in a rash of tears, done away with in the flowing blood, the earth heaving none, still as ice. I'll dance the jig of the dragonfly, a glass or two, I'll dance alone, I will. It'll be the lights blinding me, I'll stand in the headlights, coming away, no, coming apart, there'll still be nothing, I'll come apart and I'll go, there'll be less and less of it, so I predict, yet I am forever wrong. Ah lapse, sweet collapse of naught, I'll be in-dreaming, there, what of it, spasm, I might forget. Come and go as you may please there's nowhere to come to, nowhere to go, I can't. Still, these dead roads, a stretch of grass, fresh-cut grass, dead birds falling flaming from the sky, no, it won't matter, no. Head of dust, I'll see to that, it's been noted, head of dust and ashen silenced. No speech now there'll be the shaking of the hands and the winds gathering silently, blowing the smoke I exhale away into some foreign distance. That'll be the toll, taking my breath away. Ah the traces collapse into empty sands, the skin cracked, perhaps I'll smile, perhaps I'll permit myself. All in all, a dog barks, it is raining again, wandering here afar, stagnant, the night almost laughs, silently, I'll laugh too, we'll have a jig, death and I, always did, always will, until the final close...

...Ah, lighten up or you'll choke, there'll be shit in your eye, there'll be the sting of the asp, some soundless echoing, dance away, dance onward. I'll know no bounds, it's noted, speeches of the lost, the residues of time and the absence of sound. Only the music of the skull, the polka of the damned, away with that, you'll say, I say no, not ever. The bones shimmering with the heat of the soil, that's how it is, leave it be for now, impossible to miss. What's that now, drunken?, folly again, follow the ladder down, there are snakes in the grass, they'll show you the way to immobility, shadow of a thankless night. There'll be no-one in the haze, through the sky no white chariots, that's for the dreamers, the allotment pickers, the never having lived a drop of the blood, yes, they have nothing to do with me. So on it goes, happens to us all, so they say, birthed just the same, that's all that matters, dying with a flourish or out of nothing, let it be. Nothing, again, well stick a needle in your arm then, drink up your jug, empty it all, emptiness following in upon emptiness. What a time was never had, who really recalls, I can't recall. Dead all of your goddamn days, dead of this, bludgeoned by this, raped by this, turned to stone, ash, and insane by this. The curtains drawn or torn down, they'll just be replaced, blood red of course, carry me home, no, I have no home, it's settled now, it's been burned down, I was never there...

...Ah the hole in your head, the sky, sky of vertiginous beauty, traceless and untouchable, I'll just sit here with my bottle, I won't move, I'll watch the stars, no Absinthe, no, not like Van Gogh, poor bastard, trying to drown himself with paint, they killed him, ah a severed ear is nothing to a man of the world, what's the problem?, they still killed him. I'll stick to my dying, nothing else, more or less, not much, not much happening, all the while the growing and the dying, yes the growing is the dying, ha-ha, sit there, drink your drink and shut up. Nothing now. I can't. I can't go on. There's nothing to it. I could...But no...

...Ah the whores, they were out tonight on the promenade, I almost choked on my laughter. An auld fucker like me, staggering, half-lost, they'd have robbed me blind and the Caribinierri, well, they'd have probably laughed until they shat themselves at me and the condition of me, drunk and dishevelled, and not a note in my wallet, smeared with lipstick from some gristle bone and flesh. No I just kept walking, that was enough to contend with. Back to my shadow upon the wall and the half-light of the candle and the headlights searching the walls and then across the ceiling. Yes, the silence of it, blessed, no more the vile ugliness of it until another day. Ah what's to be done, I can't recall, I'll say it's nothing, septic, all over again, so much the pity, the long shadow drawn out. I masturbated violently into some tissue, then I just lay there vacantly on the bed. I thought about nothing, I was a vague sky. Afterwards, death entered in like a chill...

...If I spoke, if I ever, no good, I can't foresee it, plain sailing all the way, past this and that, through that which, in-dreaming, close the door I'd say, that would be the marvel, hanging my head in slumber. No rest for the living, fuck the wicked, they'll dance, of course. Yet if I spoke, from the mouth, this gaping hole in my face, what of it, I could never, there might be blood, I might investigate that, always do, it's noted, I'll do it again. Yet if I ever spoke again, there'd be a forest fire, I might collapse, lapse, I might pass out, having spoken, what words could come. It'd be all in the wind, it might catch the back of the head of someone walking down the street ahead of me, a fish-wife of a lie, there, no words, vacant echoes by the time they pass from the old muscle to the throat, so I might not, I never will, no nothing, under the breath, how now the speeches, different from words, naughts and crosses, nothing in the hands, ah why did I begin, nothing much of it, far too much, the worms will have me yet, I'm done, first thing this morning as I lay there, not having slept a wink, I lay there, I listened, I'm done in again...

...Dread head and spasm lock, back to the old mid-day table with the bottle again, I was bred for doing nothing, ha-ha. Ah the splendour of it, it greases the wheels, (any old cliché will do), ah my time flowing down the pissoir-mouth of death, I care not, neither broken, spun out of kilter, sun of my mad dreaming, I say, I say it again. Ah this morning's concession like a balm, like the laughter of the blazing night, I'll never know, I might pace around in here a little, perhaps take a piss, wait for my meal, hungry today, yes, I could love, even, a fool's game fit for nothing, yet why not, what could be the loss, I'm not going anywhere, nothing much, nothing much is happening, afar, all afar, never knowing, as if the distance mattered. Only to the living, the dead don't have the dignity to roar up at us from their silent quarters, screaming, *All is a lie!*, just so we'd know. Yet some do, not many, no not so many, I've nothing to lose, frozen pain or no frozen pain, in or out of this, back to from where before, yes, all is loss, taken from afar, it wouldn't kill me, I'm more likely to do it myself, with the to and fro and the silences, no nothing, head in a sky of wilted flowers, their colours erased, bleeding into nothing more. No nothing doing, no, I'll drain another glass...

#5 ...I'll begin again...No, no matter that's of no use to anyone, least of all me, I couldn't, I'll choke it out yet, there might be. I could leave, little bloody wonder, somewhere between the living and the dying, I'll pass, I'll laugh it off, there'll be night in me yet, always night, colourless. They say black is no colour, well then, so be it, I am colourless. No sense in going, I've come too far to leave, deft, alone, bulk, scarlet sky of wordless tide. Strange that the blood will cease, I'll dwell on that, half a pulse's step nearer to the end, what then, nothing. Well tiptoe through the tulips, avec moi, I spat out my wine thinking of that one again, like a child, I almost choked on myself. Yes, nowhere, here, I haven't spoken in days, no matter. Ah, we're duped by speech into the calamity of it, said once too often, gathering bones, spreading the slurry of it, of the illusion, duped, one and all, it's noted. Well call colours, voluptuous walls closing in, often, nothing new there, whispers, vapours of memory, vertigo night of empty spit. Time is not going anywhere, I say, I am time, that's absurd, I can't be, I am time going nowhere, for all to see and for me to see in all of them. How terribly dull, bloated, grotesque, well-trained, yes. Begin again from what?, a failed sense?, speaking at large?, plumage?, some sun? -I'd rather just sit here with my jug, laugh to myself quietly of the nothing. Ah, there's really no use in this, heave-ho once again, spectre and salt and the bound tongue, I'll drown yet. No. No inclination to that, almost did, once. All of this living and the dying is so jaded, I'd tear out the spleen of it, if it had a spleen, doubtful, head in this silence that I detest or love, death or no death. For all eternity, they say. I can't imagine, vampirical, all of your days spent screaming for an ever-higher death, up there, they say it's heaven, who knows, blind faith, the ever-lasting bliss of love. I'd be sick, I'd be vomiting constantly, they'd cast me out, I'd laugh, they would, I'd be glad, nothing here I'd say, you've been duped, you've been lied to. Daylight screams viciously enough, that's what blackens, I'll think of the horses, I'll sit here in my room, vaguely, am I really here, have I been here before, no, not a bloody arse's chance, I'd know. Perhaps not? Not a chance. Begin again, these are the words of a fool, all dead, all done, not dead enough, there's always a way, why would I bother...No, no not enough...

...Lest I say and to be done with it, much of the here and to the fro, it's noted, the bulk of it, a trunk full of rats, stench higher, rise higher, laughter long, dying, dying as if to burn there'll be a flaming clown yet, he'll strip the light to shreds. Who'll fall or not, that might concern the flight of some spasm and the breaking bone of the sky's limits unknown, carried across, where, I'll laugh yet there'll be nothing worth laughing about, no, my eyes peering out of the dead darkness, looking for no other, silenced all, let them be so. Nothing much of the skulk lest there be charity unshadowed by emptiness, dreaming less and less and from what folly, scars on my eyelids. No, nothing, blend with the night and become shadows of the empty moon, a deft dragoon of sullen artifice. We'll dream, I'll dream, never having slept and forever alone, but one, that counts, I can't stop being, I can. Again, again a mortuary's tears and the slug of it, the piecemeal drapery of it, the room ablaze with shadow, flesh falling away to ash, I can see it all, I'll never leave it be, back again, this way or that, until the end, it seems such waste, words and nothing more, thoughts and nothing more, no meaning, enough they say, joy in this and that, I say it again, I'll say nothing much, no, nothing at all, let it go...

...The last cascade of the sunken eye, long to fall, yes, in the splendour of some thankless breath. Where now my cadaver, what business to attend to, no, only the one and all. The sunk skull in the half-light once again, it might roll off, I might burst a blood-vessel, think of it, I'm through, death through the shoulder-blades, no nothing majestic, horse teeth beneath a vacant moon and the untied flesh of having been bound to the coil, lapse of worthless silences, absences in the throes of the wordless fathom. I say no, fuck that, fuck all of it, nothing new, I will not say it again, fuck it, I say. Ah I can barely breath, I curse the breath of this, of this being or not being, never one nor the other, else. Where now the laughter, slaughtered am I, king of nothing, a god, a naked wind, an open grave, sunk dead and breathless, I watch the air, I'll make a cross of it yet, all of this. It's noted, what from my inactivity, nothing there, I'll breathe, that'll be enough, I'll shit cum and piss and that will suffice, no hands upon me, no loss, breaking my own bones willingly. I'll stick to my jug of blood, that will suffice, let it never run dry. Ah no I'm not bitter can't you see there's nothing there much or else but the fragmented silences and the coming and the going and the toing and the froing, spectral all, dead space undone, stretching. Still the noose, perhaps I'll make one, just to test myself, or perhaps I'll hang it in the window, a fine shadow, I'll laugh, like Christmas decoration, ha-ha. I'll never begin again. There's nothing to run from, I'll stay here, it's noted...

...Ah the days, come what may, what could be better or worse, there's no comparison, I'll fade, whittled down purpose, I exist for none, it's noted, it has been. Meanwhile the birds scatter in flocks across the cerulean blue sky, I could almost walk the promenade, but no, too drunk and sick, down the hatch, as they say, no better, in a little while, almost. The tears may come, I'll start off weeping yet end in laughter, almost always, seems that way of a gilded fashion. I know know no longer why I weep, it's senseless, yet sometimes I realise, when not in-dreaming, it's spelled out before me, this waste, that I am as wasted as the next, condemned to this. I left it all behind for this, noted yes of course, so much the spittle of having been, passing on, asking nothing of the skies. No words to take it away, and no way to give it back, ever done, ever said, some solace, the grind of the blood and the flesh vibrating. Shadow all and yes, headless, yes, without words, yes, lapse yes and blackened. Those final words, so elusive, the longing almost keeps one alive. What to say of it all, yes, yet nothing has been said of it. I say *butchery*...

#6-...Click-clack and the headless rattle of it, I'll be one and the same, foraging for naught, gathering less than spatter. Nothing new, if I did, dull dusts upon me as if I had ceased, all desires dead as floating tropical fish in a listless tank. I get to being absentee/ remembering, in a certain ghost limb fashion, as if, having stepped onwards, nothing there. The eyes are spoken for, without question, going nowhere today or for days on end, except perhaps to buy my supply of cigarettes and wine and to take the occasional meal, it's noted, again. Still now, this dead descent, no, not quite, I'm not anywhere near falling. I'll spit out of luckless shining, the skull caved in as if by a rock -no, I'll not, there'll be nothing of that. The skull caved in by distances, fruitless again, back to the corner of the room, smoking in my way, drinking my jug, all romance dead to the breath of hell, some kind of echoing prank played upon oneself, no, not now, broken valves of feeling, absence -*ad infinitum*...

...All day by day, ah the bask of it, catching oneself off guard, seeping like an infected wound, in the lightless sun, murk and emptiness. The window there and all for me to see, if I could, yes, I'll make it to the chair, from the bed where else, careful now, dead hands make lighter work. No good, ah the disgust of it, no, I'll stay, I'll drink my glass, there'll be some solace, from what I'm unsure. It's myself, or perhaps the other, drifting alone, like the vacant sky above. I'll clamber for nothing nor for no man, I'd as soon set it all alight, drought then, heaving of sky thicket, scattering the teeth of silence, emptying out the all and the all of none, undone. Flush with this or that, no sense there anyhow, rambling like an old man, a prime rib of emptiness, flesh searing in the depths of the desire to erase all, full tilt, no, not for this day or perhaps for that. No, the days have ceased to matter, the delineation of what, some circus, dark or not, I'm steady, what of it. All the while, all the while the whispers, vapours and voices, they speak of nothing, futility has it's own language. Ah now, I can't remember, there'll be hell to pay, drive the bull from the fields, there'll be some kind of, no, there'll be nothing at all, it's noted, I'll spit out blood in the mornings, I'll laugh, not knowing of what I am laughing. That's the ticket, I'll say it again, a fucking parrot, that's what I'm becoming, drenched in shite, over again, all of this over again, I can't leave it alone, I cannot leave. I do not want to leave, nothing out there but the flesh and boneyism of it, I'd rather not, in fact I insist, piss and swallow, I'll make it some other way, this way, that or naught finding the hollow sparrow's heart, I'll light my candle again, no need to explain, or perhaps I could sit here in the approaching dark, without spasm or will, here at last again, here at last, without, having everything at my disposal, without love...

...I'll say all said, hope for the best, hope for the naught and the silences of it, reeking in the hollow breath, undone by ash and nothingness, bone drought, I'll say naught again. I'll venture exile, no there was never a home, yet I'll concede, I'll resend, something else undone, for now. Anyhow where, where would I end up, if I were of a mind to leave this place. How could I leave such a festering mind behind, it would be a rare betrayal on my part, I'll disregard that. I'll make sure that I don't, a fucking disgrace, forty lashes, ha-ha. Seen rather than believed, I am, they have no idea, who, I have no idea...

(...Infidel I, that's more like it...)

...Ah tell it to the worms in the soil they won't listen, ask how I got here, just the same, ask of the breath forsaken, head in the soil also, the sun on my bare arse scalding the balls off me. Here and now, scratching at the surface of nothing left and nowhere else to be, it's decided, splendorous in-dreaming of the dark distance, against which no reprieve, scarlet longing for the absence, knowing all and nothing. I'll not go down, no I'll remember him, yes, how could I forget him, with his cracked smile and broken tombs of teeth, the blue eyes piercing, they grew silent, stone, measured out by the needle and the dropper. Sunken to death now, hollow ice to become, nothing left of to be willed nor taken nor given away, the bastard. And so little is said, I'll rage all the same till all of this is dust. Ah the jug won't claim me, I've too little to do with existing to die. One hundred thousand shadows I have known, I'll know one hundred thousand more before I swing, in the distant forests of the scattered dry ash of blood. Yes I'll swing, there's no other way, for all to see, so little to be known of. A few notebooks and so much absence, the room full of empty bottles, and me like a Christmas goose, neck limp, snapped, a stain at the crotch. Ah no it won't be of him that I'll spill my hourglass, it's of the deathliness, all that brought me here to this, at the ends of nowhere, in the first instances. Death is nothing, it has no prospects. Existence is but a wall of sound and silences and in between the in-between, the in-dreaming, the reclusion and then the vapours, traces. All tongues unravelled, all walls of the flesh torn down and done with, the breath scarred no more, the bile and vomit silenced also, drink up lest you be sickened by joy, tra-la-la...

...Something echoed, as far as I can tell, I'll say nothing, there won't be a whisper said of it. Yet today, out there, nothing, today's nothing was far from notable. I can't even, no, no I can't bring myself, what use. That'll be the spine warping, it's noted, yes, what I said, all that has been said, no, no that's untrue, I was out, I stepped outside into the sunshine, granted I'd had a jug or two, no sleep as always but I'd had a jug or two. Ah the blessed vine never failed me yet, so I say, I vomited into the flowers on the promenade, some people stared, I've cared more about a shit I have taken, yes, ha-ha. I revelled in the vileness of the people, no greater disgust, no greater pleasure, no not for a man like me, yes, I am appalled by love. All the same the humidity almost killed me and I longed to be back again, all the way, all the way down the promenade. I took refuge in a café. I'll sit here, I thought to myself, I'll sit here with my dark glasses on, cane at my side, funny how I was helped to my table and chair, I laughed to myself. I was in full view of the promenade and the beach and the ocean, I could hear it, a choir of angels to the senses -ah spit! The café was animated, I drank my wine with haste, smoked, I even ventured to remove my dark glasses, feigned a blind man, rolled my eyeballs aimlessly. Well it wasn't noted all that much, it was all for appearances anyhow, nothing of it. Ah, the balm of the wretched, speaking without significance, the ever-dead. Still as I became drunk the tears welled, thousands of years to come to this disaster, how perversely beautiful, I laughed suddenly to myself at the realization that this was perfectly acceptable for many. I laughed so forcefully that I vomited on myself, it was beyond my control, I swept the bottle of wine and the glass from the table in a fit of hysteria, they crashed, I snatched up my cane, staggered, nudged past a few incoming customers, brushing the vomit off my chest, to a chorus of oohs and ahs. I cursed the bastards, wavered, fell headlong into a bush outside the café, legs struggling to find concrete once again like an overturned insect. I'll make it yet, I said to myself, I did. Yes, incidental, so much of the nothing about it, swine all of them - *ah to be a butcher!*...

#7-...I'll say it again, headlong into the rapture of it, lest I be misunderstood, into the rapture of despair. No no, no other way to bend a bone or two, forgetting the voices claiming speech, drought or not, calling you on. They remain stationary. I say breathe as little as possible, wait your turn, listen no more to the shimmering sunlight of it, fall in or out/ fall out and be done with it all, to fall deaf, blind, numb in the pageantry of the scalded meat, twice removed from all that could ever be, nettle thrashed and so again. Say nevermore, not once, I'll just, in spite of that, or else, coloured less and less by questioning, say nevermore, not again. Ah spill your bile you'll be nothing but slurry in the end, where's the worth in that, it's perfection. No nothing then, no, having taken it all away, no release, no, how could one sense it, a ridiculous posture. It comes soon enough, a myriad of claims and then but one, often wondering of how, never having limb by limbed, stretched out, to be done with them, to be done with all of this, I'll say I might. It's all so bloody tiresome either way, the waiting, reduced to waiting by no other climate. Ah the lungs of it, the heart of it, the severed cortex of a smiling in the dark. Yes, what's rot, dancing teeth, and the polka of despair drilling into the skull day by day. I suppose I could, nothing doing, no, forget it, I don't want to listen yet I can't stop any of it. I'll bury my head in the pillow, I'll punch these walls in order to re-align myself. I'll think of my being erased, how bloody tiresome, it's all so blatant that it's tiresome, dusts sand and misery, again, drying blood and so on it goes, no, there's no way out of this vile sequence. Yes, an adagio of nothingness, an orchestra of shit, hollowed out, jugular, neck snapped, hands finally silenced. The raging around in prisons to crack the shell of death, failing once again, once again the eternal recurrence, it seems so, no poison so sweet, misery damned misery. I'd tear it all to shreds, I'd wipe my arse with it. Still, no use in that, I'd probably laugh myself sick, a dead stillness always comes after such matters. Away again once more, away, sudden now, the noose still hanging above the window, peasants all, all of them, and me more dead/ alive than the lot. No refrain, no loss to me, my gain in fact, sweet rapture of despair, my bollocks, what a jangle of shit...

...Over again, under again/ see-saw/ out of which/ well still as if not notion/ placement/ placement of the old wounds/ jaggering up again to stifle/ nothing left to stifle...All the same and all done with/ sleeping none/ knuckles bruised in reclusion/ a prize fight/ shadow-boxing with Time/ no contest/ I failed and the blood smears on the bare white walls. No there was never any way, hands bandaged, tears streaming down the face, sitting here, glass in hand, cigarette burning in ash-tray, streets empty, no sound, not a step, not an echo, not a whisper, nothing noted. A dead bird in the hand and two in the bush ablaze, wailing carcass of love, whispering now how's your father, stings a little, doesn't it. Done in and undone, crawl lest your limbs warp with the weight of it, out of socket and blind death, night now, forever night, the street-lamps lit, the room illumined, no flickering candle, empty breath empty echoings, nowhere, out of which the nothing births, in-dreaming, in between the coming and the going, still the heart, still the birthing of the final, each laughter comes heavy, nothing noted, nothing said, I'll speak to myself, then, no, nothing spoken, nothing, nothing, a foreign abandon, an empty solace, I can hear the ocean yet not a sound, I'll...

...Ah to lay it all down for nothing's sake, unto naught, trace of the night's liquid, unlike tears. Bled sun/ void of fallen burning waste, head above water, the waters are ablaze, no nothing, lack and breaking without sweat, time and locked to the bone, disfigured night calling on the breath of the wretched, a sickly parade, a rogue atrophy, eyes erased, skull of one thousand absences, I'll sever yet, no sense in coming or going now, back or unto again, dreaming less and less of the pull of the tide/ absurd/ extractions of teeth/ leprous meat of a corrupt endless/ bone writhe of stupor, it's noted/ singing headlong into the void with what colours this nothingness my blackened cheer/ vibrating narrow and the poison of the cleft viper, stray along, waste naught, sing less. Ah it's all the same willed or not stripping the skin away, lingering on the inherent waste. Some silence in that and the pale stagger, long stirred, finalised, birthed or not anything more than lessened. Weaving to this and that, I'll snare myself less and less, with more and more of nothing, voracity, much or else being, subtle harsh or breathing less my sun my laughter. I'll snuff out the light, this trick of the light that I am, I'll collapse into amber, dissipate, what. Knowing now and how it all, if ever, scattering dust across the room, I'll go where the hidden chalice burns, yet there'll be nothing there, I won't recall anyhow. Vaulted, unrest of the tongue/ splice again the bone's listless carrion, stink retch of cold hands, my death. Going on, yes, there's little else, there's nothing else, illusions of thoughts and the desert of consequences. There'll be blood in the dropper yet, like a summer bloom, stealing back the horror with the addition of fresh horrors. It'll have to go, no more of this, I can't leave I'm too indifferent to stay in this shit. I can't remember how I came here, no use all the same, drink up your jug and dance the dance of the noose's chamber. I am condemned, no nothing new in that, I'm repeating myself, a circus pageantry of raging wounds. Bled out, tears for what, no I won't go on, I'll be stubborn, nothing will not claim me, the teeth will rage in a jack-knife of death, rock-a-bye-baby, all done with, the voices, the echoes, the whispers, the whores, I'll sleep yet, a corpse of aspiration, I'll never sleep, I'll sleep now, where now my noose, it's noted, not a trace, it's final......

...Ah, what piss-luck...No luck, or there's some manner of a jangle here, I'll just lie here...Oh Christ, my head, and me with the feckin' noose still around my neck...No, no bloody luck and me at the end of my tether, as if I could be otherwise, and the rail torn out of the wall, no, it wouldn't hold the weight of me, worse it gets...Better still, once the chair was kicked away, what a weight, all of my weariness like a pregnant sloth, whatever that means...I was fit for it, Christ, I was fit for it, I'll have to make sure it's noted, so no-one will understand...Ah well, it's the first sleep I've had in weeks, a strange gift, I'll laugh about it yet...And me with the rope-burns on my neck, I'll probably bruise, ah yes, that'll teach them, the bastards, that'll give them something to stare at, if I ever...No no great revelations, I merely blacked out, the breath sucked out of me and the blood to the head bursting like a fucked heart...Incidentally enough, it's daylight, the shutters closed, ah Christ the failure of it, what kind of idiot am I...Ah yes the jug, I'll blame the jug, where now my jug that caused such imprecision...And a smoke, Jesus, I'm coming alive again, no that's of no use, no...Ah yes, nothing claimed nor lost in the briars of it, hollow the sound all the same, deafening even, I'll have to...Right, up and at it again you old dirt-bag, there's flesh on those bones yet, yes...

...Ah back to my table and the heave-ho of it, jug half-drained, smoking like there's nothing left of me, and on I go. Ah that's the...torn up...no that's the ticket torn up, all over and again, I need that. Nothing claiming and yet what a foothold, stagnant no, too fresh from that, somehow. Ah sure it's noted I exist for nothing, a porous wound all the same, scarab, desert plains and the knowledge of scattered bones. I owe my guilt to no-one, or no-thing, I'll dance in the flaming shit of it, a song perhaps, somewhere else, scattered afar. What now, what words consoling the endless dark, fissures be damned, I'll go, no, I mean relieve myself...It's noted...No, no revelation nor a new beginning clinging to the life I almost erased. I see the shit-stained teeth of all things, gather me less or not in the midst of the amber sunlight. Days, nights, back again, a bruise at the temple, nowhere again, no not now, yes again, nowhere again, what a cunt this is. Back then and of that to follow, unto naught, elapsed, breathen fallen, sunk dead wretch of grandeur, pitch of sun, nothing wasted, I'll just sit here, it's noted. Well turn the screw in my eye, that's how it evolves, sink fast, drag, something, a dead hand offering sweets from a casket. Funny how the puppeteers play, I remember, the wonder of it took me, a child scared in a room with no way out or back, and I am still, no, out there is the death of me, it's true, I'd rather smash my fingers with a malette, and then some, taking back the breathing silk of silent words, dreaming less and less, the poetry of it, set to light. I'll never know much beyond nothing much worse than this, it's noted. I'll take whatever, no not the sun, I'll take the night, the collapse of it, the...No words for today, no not a murmur of it, yet they keep coming, from what distance, measured by what and how. No smiles for today. The bloody noose still around my neck. Sonorous, I'll wait...

#8- ...All alack, alack...Faceless...The bruised knuckles blossom into thorns of heavy speech, deathly white time and the vertigo of a thankless breathing. Aside, left or right or back again, beginnings of the pissoir, echoings, echoing out down there, head sunk and all aglow, birthing silences, silences...It'll occur to me yet, or perhaps it never will, some strain, into the shadows, yes, into the shadows, curled up, tongue dry, orbiting myself. I'll do the Fandango yet, ha-ha, yes, I'll make merry a little for none other but myself. Ah, there are so many possibilities for a dead man. I'll can still play at the cardiac arrest, anon, no way back, no, not ever. Cascading into a graven face, without form, no, that's not plausible, as if I ever believed in it. Ah, the Harpies have got me now, as if you haven't noticed, as if they weren't there before -you'd swear I killed a man or something so bloody insignificant as that! Not a step, not a glance, no, the ceiling looks just fine from my cot, I'll lay here and stare awhile, I'll not move for a...No...Up and make life difficult for yourself like you always do, I say to myself, the hilarity of it, often. Another jug to be filled, a thirst in me like one thousand desert plains, no sound, perhaps some vultures circling. Well perhaps some birds, tweet-tweet, there they go, there that's it explained to you, just in case, who's in case?, it's noted. Christ I'm some eejit, with this whole 'it's noted' business, slow today to be sure, I can't look. So much for that. Toing and froing. About face. In the mirror, the bruising is there alright, almost beautiful, a deep crimson around the neck with tinges of stale yellow, aches a little, still. Ah well, add it to the collection, the bloated liver, there'll be nothing spoken of it, unless I...

...Today now no different, difficulties done with, or so I think, flames subsided, ash in the mouth, a wasp-sting of a day where nothing burns you, the ennui, long shadow, fierce, absence of disarray, knowing no way past the door, closed to all, none ever coming to take me away, take me out, and of it I care not a fragment, I'll let it go to dust. Ah the swagger of the old days, the trick of the light of youth, no doubt, sticks in the throat like a chicken bone after a fine feast, a famine now, yet. No, no prospects, none wanted, none believed, nothing to gain, so I've come to pass, not quite, bled out, not quite, echoing, echoing, always echoing. Sun of a dead heart bleeding not, I'll say, with what a flourish, as if to sink the gods, as if I could, as if -what an interminable reference of claims, vanity all! I'll have my eyes out yet, some doubt to grace the stage of it, they'll sizzle in the pan, I'll have them out, I will. I'll stagger for the dark glasses then, the cane, the blood streaming down my face, what a spectacle I'd be, almost, as if, no, no reason or rhyme to that. Ah, it's all gone not a bit of life to it, and me not yet broken, without hopes, prayers or thoughts of the day in hand. No not dead yet but not far to go, and the sting in the throat, ah, nothing to be made of that, the noose cast aside in the corner like an unwanted child's toy -Get thee hence!, I said, and it was done with. Like a coiled dead serpent it lies there in the corner, lifeless, the neck aching just a bit. Lucky?, no. Yet I could have lain there for days on the floor, half-snapped, bone fractured, groaning like an old woman with the cancer without the Morphine. Ah, it's all a bucket of sunshine, sandcastles, bollocks and dead flowers scattered over me, but yes ah yes there was a sleep like I have not known in years. A strange thing to be judge, jury and executioner of oneself, the head astray, dreaming of the nothingness, the absence of oneself in the universe. Beyond all time. Not a stitch. Obvious really. Unfettered, unmoved. No consolations. Just the cold dead stretch, and then naught, it's good enough a reason to snap the bones, seek out the silence, the unknowing rot...All is stagnant, all is not...

...Well enough of the jug for now, the dilly-dallying, we'll stretch the legs, no not like on the Cross, a taste of something unlike the breathless air of this hovel, a stroll and perhaps a bite, that'll do, might as well, the glasses and the cane as always. Out we go then, heave-ho and the jangle of it, the jingle jangle the auld triangle of it, I'm hardly imprisoned. Shave away and do the bullock no harm, enraptured, some sense of, no not ever of, I'll die of, all the while I'll, no...Ah stop going on about the coming and the going, you'll bleed yourself dry of it, and what's more. Out!, and be done with this. Do you have your cane?, (Yes, I have my cane), And your dark glasses?, (Yes I have my glasses), ah Christ, on it goes, Have you your shoes and socks on you?, (Yes, I have my shoes and socks on me), Have you tied your laces, combed your hair and washed your face? (-Ah feck off Mammy!). Good, and to be gone with all of that, the bitch...Ah well, yes, all the same...I believe there is a Carnival on the pier tonight, I'll take a flask of the fire-water, that'll be the ticket. Ah, the joviality of the young, so unaware of the searing blade at the throat, some may never even...I'll fold the cane for a bit yet, head for the promenade, ditch the glasses in the afternoon light, I'll be a radish, radish red in the raw sunlight amongst all these caramel bambini's of easy living, and me with the red raw arse of suffering, the bruised neck and the silence of it. -Vai!, -Vai!, -Andiamo!, and out into the sunlight, out of debt for now, having tried and having failed, nothing new in that but sure there's failure in all things...

...Ah cast out un-snared into the animal wilderness, ah out into the weight of it. The intoxication of the crowd, every pulsing heart and flesh and mind, the colours of the spectrum, here I find myself, almost, almost as if there were something to it, meaningless all and yet how the sky is smeared with so many colours, the buzz of the crickets, the scents, the variety, I'm almost alive again, I tell myself. Well a drink is order your Lord your worship, a jug or two, we'll settle by the ocean, on the promenade, I could almost...Here a table, there a table, everywhere a... A thick-haired woman sits filing her fingernails at the table next to me. Promptly, I'm brought a jug of fine wine, no expense spared, ah the waitresses are even beautiful, white blouses open, tight black skirts, I could stare at their arses all day long without a stir in these drying loins, yet. No, I am a shadow here, I came to nowhere out of nowhere, I gaze at the sun. I'll sit here for a time, perhaps another jug, collar pulled up to hide the noose marks, the cravat should do it. A composite gentleman. Man of the world, ha-ha. Ah, the illusions we create in the midst of the many, gestural, breathing calmly, all the while...Asunder unto naught...A swine writhing in the inglorious shit of it, nothing harboured, ha-ha, as if I could utter such a thing, what with these lungs and tongue and the scattering of the evening birds back out to the sea. I'll just sit here, drink away and drink ho, observe the nothing of all of this, this charade, I'll smoke and it's noted...

...Belly-up, what for the drowning of it, and the forever forgetting. Dragged out, it was I, I who dragged the long shadow into this I know. And I thought, as if it could be, oh how we fool ourselves, how I deceived myself, yes and no, on and off, ah spit. No, now I must, I came here now I must, I do not wish to but I must, this carnival, these Roman candles in the sky, the screams and the bustle, no, not for a man like me, not with my disposition, bastards, all of them. Dark now, and the whir and click of the machines and the lights, I can't see straight, I'll walk yet I'll cascade a little, left or right. I'll clear my own path, a few curse -Ah away and fuck yourselves!, I say, they don't understand and I'm not one for interpreting anyway, no, not for me, all of this candy-floss and popcorn and the absence of the jug. Must I die of man? Acrobatics and the spitting of flames, what a useless business, horrid, and the contortionists, the clowns, if I was ten years younger there would be fucking trouble! Ah, back into my despair mutilated by this, fucked over by this, away now, away, I am amongst the brave, so they say, I'll...The liquid flow of the evening evaporates to the death-charms of the night, better off, I say, left to the silent moorings, unsung...

#9- ...Alive again?, my arse... What a shackle...Too much of the jug last night and yet still no bloody sleep. Wretched today, I deserve a decent flogging and no mistake, to have set myself to dreaming in the midst of -*that!* What an act of criminality, what waste and so little time left to suffer gladly at the hands of my own self. No, never again, I'll be no lap-dog, they'll have me dead yet, can't you see it? It's of them that I am dying, of them that I have burned unto this place of death and rupture. Enough, enough now, all said and done. I can't live, there's nowhere, I can't breathe, I can't step, I can't...It's noted, it's noted, it's noted, it's bloody well noted over and over again and me with the...what? Nothing...No no, there's no poverty to it, I'll enrich the soil yet there's no poverty to it, someday, a dance with the night, her arms and her charms lest there be else to follow. Ah such a waste all of this, no, not I, this insufferable indescribable, this writhing all over with an insect/ spasm shock electrical eel of a writhe -*ah fucking spit!* I'll have to wash it all off me, I'll scrub, that's what I'll do, I'm soiled by them, I'm sickened, I'll vomit, I am sickened enough to eat my own shit at such a lifeless disgrace that I've been torn into. I'll bring the jug to the bath. I'll drink and I'll find some succour. I'll pass an hour, no sound in there but for the fan going. Bastards all, I can't breathe, my head is swimming -no I won't laugh it off!, there are sharks beneath the surface -I'll go gladly to them! Over and under. What? Headless regeneration, and me in the stocks covered in rotten fruit and mards. I'll run the waters, there now, easy now, drink your jug, drink your jug and wait...

...Ah let me tell you about her, briefly mind, I might as well, there were a few but none like her, not in any estimation, how could there be? I was younger then, much younger and less bloated with the pox, the riddle still fresh, the mind turning, my head stuffed with bookish things and smears of paint. Dublin was not of the rare auld times, it was, well, how shall I put it?, as bad as everywhere else?, yet not the same, the jangle, the absurdity was absent. And me sure nothing new there, gallowing down the whiskey and wine, every last coffer pissed to the winds. I lived alone, a small room, shared toilet/ bathroom, rampant mice in winter in those old tenement buildings like nowhere else. Rathmines was...a freedom of a sort, and the grief of the final breath exhaled, the lungs rotted out of him, a good friend to be sure, I'd never seen such brutal horror, nor since. Ah yet that was no excuse, I was as life-willing as I am now, as if I have gorged myself to the point of unbearable sickness, laughter not, I'll splice, I'll stray. All the same, yes, she, her, her name was E., (no, not you, you bitch, in case you ever come across this, ha-ha). Well, staggering out of where what or neverland, gallon drunk, steady now, yes, full, it must have been about two a.m. I finally get to my street anyhow, Leinster Rd., and there she is, laying there in the middle of the road, crossing and uncrossing her legs, the knees of her black tights torn, black brogues and a black dress, thin, a shock of wild black hair. Well she's murmuring away to herself, head rolling from side to side, not an idea, not a fucking venture of an idea what she's saying as I approach. Then I see the black eyes, the burst lip, silenced. No cars on the road really in this area at this time of night, but some eejit could have made shit of her without question. Anyhow, I get down on one knee beside her, the eyes rolling in her head, the reek of stale whiskey off her could have flattened a stampede. No point in asking the young lady is she alright, not a step. I gather her up slowly onto my shoulder. Hardly a pick on her. Light as hollow bones. A short walk. She's out for it. I reach the tenement, thank Christ for the summer nights, I think to myself. Up the steps and fumbling for the key into the lock and into the door, no sound no trace, they're all drunks in the building anyhow, not a leg to stand on. Down the corridor. No sound but the key in the door and her breathing. Inside. Light switch. I lay her down gently onto the bed to the right of the door. She's in bad shape alright, Christ, she must have took some hiding, the eyes of her, the same colour as the noose's marks on my neck. I sit down in a chair by the window, the shutters semi-closed, letting in shafts of light from the street-lamps. I uncork a bottle, take a deep swallow, light a smoke and exhale into the room...

...Alright I sit there, watching her, staring out onto the street, the usual scenes that time of night, a few drunks staggering up the road, kicking over rubbish bins, tra-la-...no. Every once in a while I check to see if she's breathing. She rolls over and ah Jesus, there's a bloodstain where her crotch had been on the quilt. I reel back, almost vomit in the sink. Nothing to be gained by waking her now, no. She's in a deep one, but every now and then a convulsion of sorts. This is the way of it, I think, and now what. I light a smoke and pace around the room, swigging from the bottle. Time and nothing else, dark shadows, the room ablaze with anguish, mine and hers silenced by the out. Mine is nothing, of nothing, I know nothing of this, I am no man, a child, worse, ragged sun. Ragged sun breaking now, just after 5 a.m. I'm next to nothing, drunk, wired, I didn't sleep back then either. Still, there's plenty of wine, welfare cheque the previous day. What now?, what could be worse for her, violated, she'll have to wake up to this. Jesus she's beautiful. A waif. Her knees are raw from falling about the street no doubt. No point in calling the filth, they never do anything, they'd probably blame her, or perhaps me, how did she get here, well I carried her, I know nothing...Ah Christ, what a jangle, she'll have to...I'll...

...I sit on the edge of the bed, watching the rise and fall of her, drinking from the bottle, I was less refined then, no jug in those days, just straight down into the gullet. Smoke away. I keep looking at the bloodstain, about the size of a large fist. Ah, this is for the dogs, what a feckin' nightmare, no not for me, but for the poor girl, she took some beating, and more. I'll have to wake her, I can't, I try again, she murmurs, oblivious, moves to stretch as if I were a familiar hand that was trying to rouse her. Then the shock/ recognition of not recognising her surroundings, nor the hand nor the face that's before her. She jolts back suddenly into the corner of the bed, back to the wall, like a frightened cat, eyes wide through bruised flesh, terror. I throw the covers over and try and hide the bloodstain, but no. Take a drink of this, I tell her, offering her the bottle. She downs a good third, straight off, no question, a slight trickle of it runs down the side of her swollen mouth which she wipes with the felt sleeve of her dress. I tell her where I found her, she has no recollection. I ask her her name. She tells me it is E. I offer her a smoke and she takes one, nicotine-stained fingers all quivering, I light her up. I tell her that she can stay with me until she's healed but that she might need medical attention if the bleeding doesn't stop. She nods her head, exhales, she has another hit from the bottle, passes it back to me. Her voice is soft, she's well-spoken, not gutter-trash, eloquent. E. starts cracking her knuckles anxiously. I don't ask any questions. She'll speak if and when she's ready. She starts to cry but it is obvious that she doesn't want to be touched. I ask her does she want something to eat, but she doesn't hear me. She's elsewhere, in-dreaming. We sit there and pass the bottles and cigarettes back and forth until she lays down and falls asleep again...

...Time passes, yes it does that, I always had no sense of it, never cared for it, but anyhow. She's been asleep for an eternity it seems, yet nothing of that, I'm still drinking, I know nothing of what to do next. Ah the pox of this, some fucking animal, I'd cut his throat. She rolls over to face the room, slowly levers herself up, head heavy and lowered, feet upon the floor. Blinds still drawn I ask her if she'd like the light in, she says no, no thank you. A bite to eat?, she shakes her head. She asks me for a drink, I stand and walk over to her with a fresh-opened bottle, she takes it gently, drains a good draw of it. E. sits there vacantly staring at the floor, hair over her face without sound, breathing slowly. I ask her what she wants to do, she says she doesn't know, she can't remember what happened, or moreso won't, I wouldn't either. I give her a smoke and with a shaky hand she accepts, she hasn't yet seen her face, Jesus he/ they beat the shit out of her, as well as the rest. She has such beautiful eyes beneath the swelling, the bruised flesh, there's a strange stillness there, no pain, in spite of what's happened. E. stands up, kicks off her heels, walks over to the table where I am sat and sits down facing me, the sun streaming in through the gaps in the blinds cuts shards across her face. She asks me do I have a shower, I say no, the best I can do is a bath. She asks me will I run her one, I say I will. I stand up, waver a little, knock over some empty bottles, she's unperturbed, this is something, two damned souls in the midst of the flame, I leave the door ajar, walk down the corridor, fumble in my pocket for some loose change and slide it into the slot above the sink. Well it's clean all the same, the drunk next door cleans it daily for the price of a few jars. I run the water until it's warm, I don't add salts in case they sting the wounds. When the bath is full I walk back down the corridor, back into the room, she's still there, thank Christ...I hand her a towel...

...So I get to the notebook while she's bathing herself, that's when it all started, back then, the jangle, it's noted, all of that. No not when I met her but back then, I must have been twenty-one, head dreaming against the scars of the world, dense time, no time for anything else, scraping the flesh from the sails. No no hope then, just the ragged, the jarring, knowing nothing of the atrophy, the twist of the blade in the realms, yet knowing enough. I'm at it all the same when she comes back in, barefooted, tights in a ball and her knees raw, head lowered. Jesus, you look nearly as bad as I do, she smiles, she has a point. Still I managed to clean up the sheets, those blood-stained sheets, I hid them in the closet, no point to that laying there, I'm sure she knows. A dead man couldn't be more cynical. Yet in spite of everything, she looks somewhat renewed. I ask her if the bleeding has stopped, no sense in flogging the bush, she says yes, I leave it at that. I stand up and wash out a glass in the sink, pour her one, hand it to her and sit back down again, intact, bracket, syllabus, headless, not knowing what to do next. E. knows this. Strange that she's so calm, she tells me its okay, I can't believe she's so seemingly off-hand about this. She asks me of what I am writing, I tell her it's just a jangle of this and that, murmurs and drought, murmurs and nothing much...Ah, but we have the sunlight, she says...

...So we sit there before the window, the street, smoking and drinking, not saying much, there's nothing that can be said, me with the notebook and my skull in a dying ditch of dead birds and rotten bones. E. tells me she lives not far from here, that she lives alone, Okay, I say, we should get out of here, she agrees. Do you have any sunglasses?, she asks me. Well I know that I have a few pairs in the drawer somewhere, and as she tries them on, she's laughing as the first few pairs I give her down don't hide the bruises, but finally, one. I hate this fucking place, I tell her, but it's all that I can afford, and with me dodging work like the leprosy, she laughs out loud, sweet tones. So I pack a few bottles into my satchel, she snatches up her shoes, she's staying barefoot she tells me, I say okay. It's not far from here, she tells me, just up the road from here...

...We arrive at a large red Georgian door, much like my own. E. bangs on the door with the knocker, waits, bangs again. The sun beats down and I'm pissing wine out through my pours. Do you always wear black?, she asks me, I tell her yes. Anyhow the door opens and a large gaunt ragged man stands there, bruises of Smack use on his arms, he greets E. and steps aside for us to enter, he winks at me as we pass. Staircase to the right of the door, smell of must and cat's piss. Three storeys up and I'm almost dead, the top floor, the door a little ajar, and we're in. A round table to the left of the door, beside the singular window, E. motions for me to sit down with a wave of her hand. She lights some incense. I light a smoke. Place a bottle from the satchel on the table. E. brings over two murky glasses and sets them down in the middle of the table. I notice a coil of barbed-wire around the lampshade on the ceiling. She sits down before me, removes the sunglasses. It's evident that she's still in shock, but she seems more relaxed than I thought she might be. So we sit there in minor triumph, no not any victory, in the nothingness, silent, I am without words. E. ventures that I should lie down awhile, try and get some sleep, as always I'm in dire need of it. So we finish the bottle, I concede, I'm pretty loaded, fit for fuck all else. She slides a CD into a battered looking old stereo, Motzart's Requiem, grim stuff but soothing in its way. I set my glass down on the shelf next to the bed and look around the room: various bric-a-brac, found items, folios, it appears she is something of an artist. I feel warm. No not physically, I feel good in this den of this girl. I lay there and feel myself drifting as Lacrimosa disappears from my ears and sleep drags its shroud across me...

...Well I awaken and she's there beside me on the bed, no, I'm no saviour, she's just there and I feel her breath upon me. It's then I notice the bruise-marks on her arms, like the fellow that answered the door to us, the dead veins beneath the skin. I stare at the ceiling and wonder when last she's shot up, not a drop, not a step. I look at her lithe frame and the factuality of her addiction. I begin to wonder if this is commonplace to her, the beatings, the absences -is she whoring herself?, I don't know. She's no older than I am, at a stretch, well I haven't a ghost limb to stand on, in either respect, we'll die of one thing or another, it's irrelevant. I think to leave, I think she'll manage in her own fucked-up way just like the rest of us, but no. Disease and laughter, and the rapture of it, not an ounce of rapture in this, raped and battered for the price of a score. I pull away gently from the bed and reach the satchel without waking her, but then she's probably elsewhere. How can an alcoholic judge anyone?, one way is as good or bad as the rest, some just die more quickly and undone/ begone with this, ever to be gone. Well the sun is dying a death as I sit there at the table uncorking another bottle. Slowly. Head in a scarlet mist. Dance of nothing ever. By design. The slit wrists of desire. I watch her breathing. Something. More dead than I. Breathing still...Focus of non-time, a bloody syringe in an ashtray of spent cigarette butts, some empty plastic wrapping, a burnt bent spoon, cigarette filters scattered across the surface of the table, a clear rubber tube, citric, time erased once more. A well of rot. Curtains closing to a dead scene. I light a candle in an empty wine bottle. E. is silent. I am as alone with this as she is. I wonder if. How and what? As if. No none could ever...I'll finish the bottle and I'll leave, she's in better company now. Okay then...

#10- ...Often, I wonder afar, (always), as if dealt, or, having been dealt with the cold cut of the having severed, and all of which unto no my breath, my broken body out of dreaming, pledged to the throw of the dice once again, pillar to naught to post to headless alack, sun-drenched, spit of the damned, my sun, my star of gold my virtue; my death. Dreaming, often dreaming afar of silver silences, silver orchards, there never the sun in my dreaming, darkness only. All milk spilled now but for the ghost of it, the line, the dance, the joy of it. Headless in my world, absences and all but one, filling the depth the traces of desire, following onward, here now and in my murk, my loveless bones, once it has been said, sorrow and forever tomorrow's lack. Ah vicious collapse, no, not the floor just yet, though prone am I to lay there still on my side for hours, thinking of nothing, blood perhaps, or the erection I'll get in the casket as my body dissolves, the intestines farting and suffering without consciousness. Ah, the games, a terrible thing, consciousness. A useless fettering of a jangle, yet in the horror of it, turned in upon, gaffer of magistrate and whip, steel eye, flesh falling away it might as well do, dying before our very own eyes, soundless, yet no, perhaps a creak of sinew or ligament...Couldn't be better, on a rarefied tumour of a day, and me with the lick, the salt, and the stunned wonder of naught. And the pissing rain, belting down today and no mistake, luckily the bottles stocked up and not a care for it. An ideal day for the races, perhaps, all of them sent home, or perhaps for the promenade, no-one about, not a trace, there never is. I've walked these pissed-upon streets in glad cheer, as if in some kind of Surrealist film, a shadow, alone, unseen/ unheard, bottle in the coat-pocket, cigarette dangling, not a soul nor much of the anything else. I sit on the benches alone watching the ocean and the strand drinking quietly from my bottle of Rosso, perhaps a little thunder rumbling. The spectacle of it, and me soaked through, not a care, the hat keeping the rain from my face. Those are the days that one does not forget. There, I've said it, I know better than this nothing...

...Ah to get along, divining perhaps, retrieving for what purpose, well, better to leave things as they have never been, or noted, as if they were, pox and spit and riddle, I'll continue, yes. E., I recall I had left her there in her Heroin haze all curled up like a feline, the eyes swollen over from the bruising, and me with no idea to see her again. Well, it must have been nearly four a.m as I recall, drunk to the skies of course, thinking of it, what of it, much the same as now, yet more aware of the bite of it, the snare of it, eating me away, no silence, no surcease, no promenade then, just the winter mice but that's been noted before. Well the buzzer rings, pause, pause again, rings again more forcefully. I'm finishing off the second last bottle, so no visitors as a result. It rings again, alright, I stir, motion unto the window, stagger more like, knocking over the table, the empty bottles, ashtray and the whole bloody lot. Anyhow the window, yes, I peer through the blinds, not a trace. Gone, I say to myself...Back to the bed, collapse, stretched out. Then comes the banging on the window that almost scares the ghost right into me, like coffin-nail. Alright, again, navigation, a scattering of flowers, my graveside flowers, a table, chair knocked over and all of the rest. Well, of course it's her, rain-soaked, leaning over the railings, a bag on her shoulder. She's pissed wet, it's beating down much like those days alone at the promenade. No question of not letting her in, not in that condition, a sucker punch. I waver to the door and from the keys in my pocket open the front door to her. I step out onto the steps, motion her to come in. E. steps down from the railings and staggers over toward me. Not knowing what to say, I step inside, wait for her, lock the door behind her. Her hair is stuck to her face, mascara runs like a cruel joke from her eyes, but no tears, well. Alright then, lets get you inside, you can stay here, I say to her. Her knees are raw again as she sits down on the bed and kicks her left leg over the right one toward me. Women are alien to me, I've never known one to be other than somewhat insane, which is of course no judgement, merely my bad luck, especially back then. E. dries her hair with a towel that I hand her, tosses the towel aside on the bed and produces a bottle of Scotch from her bag, stretches it out to me. I take it as she struggles to light a damp smoke. She slumps back against the wall. She's dressed in the same black dress, black brogues, black torn tights. I sit at the table smoking, wondering what the hell she is doing here. She is without sound, eyes wild into vacant space. I'm too fucked to care. I fill two tall glasses with the Scotch, down mine and hand one to her, fill another, sit back down again. I ask her what she wants. She says that she doesn't know. Well she has no idea, and I none, and no offence but the last thing I need are junkies calling around to my room. A mess entirely. Still. I'm watching her, waiting for the works to come out and the amber fix. Yes, of course, she's been assaulted but I am no Christ, I can't save what few pennies are left of myself. So we sit there and drink our whiskey and smoke in the silence but one, the rain from outside beating against the window. All said all done, I don't need a whore calling around to my room either, with some rabid bulldog of a Pimp cutting the life out of me on account of stirring up his product. Ah to piss with it. Night without end. Ah no, no sense in turning like that, a girl in trouble, a temptress perhaps, no doubt. No harm. She'll need a score and she'll be gone, unless she's holding something. I'll stick with the Scotch, I know her terrain, but no, not anymore. Zeroed out now. Not a scratch of flesh on her. No-one coming for her here. Alright then...

...So haven said, and me with the lapse and the lice of it. Long stretch, nothing new, Jesus you get so bored you could stretch your bones with the absence of any sound in-between and far distanced, never acclimatised to it, no, not ever. Trance and the bone-barry of it, the jangle, the mesh, and all the while it's there before you, biding its time, pulsing and squirming away, meat and bone and the blood and trickle. Ah there's no use to it, shaving away the bone of it, culling the diseased animals, not a trace, spit and be gone. Use it up?, use what?, there's nothing there. Ah, the echoes, the wound there for none to see, the life there that was never lived, the drained skin of all that could ever be known of, and worse for ware, spitting columns, lacking the head when the head is needed, called upon. Noted, yes, but what of it, all sent astray all sent to where there is no sound drifting in indecent light, colours of putrescent meat, halo of the foreign blood-stained feathers of death, whispers of dread alone, whispers of the dread of being, without conviction or love, lacking the semblance of purpose, the semblance of strength, and me, I, fervent in this escapade of a room, forever staring at the absence of the world, from my dark din. Ondelay and overlay once more never without speech and yet lacking sound, elected to the one tributary, done in by reclusion, drama hunger and the lack of the onset, nothing left, nothingness, scar of ill-reason, of finality, at the end of reason. I'll sit here, yes, eyes peeling, nothing sacred or sent unto me, ah yes to remember them all and the failure of it, the lack of it, placed, never centred, what words haven to trace and the jangle of it, noted, yes. I tear out the pages and wipe my arse with them again, once again, all over again, such is the movement that I am, such is the care, and the concession -no, dead head of a ruthless sneering dreaming at the edge of the precipice, no there's nothing there, no not all over it's too much, too much the resolve, far too much the bone dust colouring of the breath, ah to be stretched finally -fuck all the seasons and the minutes and the moments and the trivial pissings of cheer. I am a dead man, I walk alone, I am death, I refute, and yes but for what of those youthful hours? I tear out the sand of my heart, I spit stray animals, all dead all done now the savagery, the brutality and the memories. I wish to disappear from my own possession, from where unto now, crawling from one stale room to the next, dreaming -nae, burning to be absent, burning to be extracted, to be ground down to the bone-meal of my dreaming, all done all finished and to be done with, screaming no more without sound, bailing out into some foreign distance, beneath skies no longer viable, the crack in the skull final, ah an axe to thresh the night from out of me, noted, feck it, lest there ever was, and I never once alone...

...I watch the morning sun ascend through the bare branches of the large tree in the driveway through the gaps in the blinds, the light cutting through the smoke-filled room. E. is unaware, her breast rises and falls, she has been in a foetal position for most of the night. The Scotch is almost finished, a bottle of uncorked wine will serve as some kind of toast to the beginning of the day when she awakens. E. will awaken to her form of nightmare and I have not been able to escape anything, death or the zone. The floor beside me is littered with torn sheets and books tossed aside. Strange the calm of insomniacal mornings, even through the haze. I notice that E. is shivering. Either junk sick or from the cold. She awakens with a start, eyes terrified, she looks at me as if I were about to murder her, retracts her body to the wall, closes her arms around her legs as if to protect herself. I realise that she has no recollection of the night before, yet wonder how she found me here; irrelevant really, I guess. I pour her a glass of Scotch, another for myself, stand up, waver a little, walk over to the bed and sit down next to her. I tell her to drink up, she'll feel better. E. downs half the glass, snatches up a packet of opened cigarettes, deals out two, I take one and from my pocket, slowly, produce a lighter. We sit and we smoke. Not a word, not a trace. I finish my drink and she hers not long after me, drops her cigarette butt into the emptied glass. Chipped black nail polish, the hands of one hundred hand-jobs, perhaps less or more, I shouldn't really, no, no room for judgement, particularly from a live-wire like me, a drunken wreck at twenty-one, and she not much younger. The silence is tangible. No, nothing, I have nothing on my mind. Her shaking comes in waves, I notice the bruises on her knuckles. She is staring away from me into the short distance of the room. I tell her, against my better judgement, that she can stay here if she needs to. Her head snaps around to meet my gaze with the mistrust of a wild feline. She asks me if she can have a bath, I say okay. I stand up, stagger over to the table again to where my loose change lies. Barely able to focus now, I find the correct coinage, I head for the door. Down the corridor. Stench of frying meat and eggs and the sound of a transistor radio. Compare and contrast. What a fucking jangle, un-noted. Okay so into the bathroom at the end of the corridor and into the slot goes the coin. I run the water...

#11...Sun envelope me and burn me dry, I say, left to my own devices there'll not be much more of this jangle. Ah, there'll be less and less conviction, more and more of this convict sense. Tally-ho!, and the worst of all possible endings shining like a silver oracle. No, I haven't forgotten the noose, nor the idiocy of it, I wear it like a crown of thorns around my neck. Stop again begin again. Let me go then, let me be forever lost, un-lost, drip-fed no more by a pale pace, here now and forever your Lord your worship. I'll have to go back to the hard stuff again. Balls to the jug, I must put away six or eight of them in a day and still no rest but for that one instance recently, half-knocked out of my perch up there amongst the damned. Yes, no, back again, a spinning-top, the bruises have faded at least. Well how much ennui can one man endure?, how much of the sunken drivel of his own self must he digest? Spitting cages, ah. Dead birds of tropical deaths, I-parrot, yes, but that's how it is, over and over with the meat-hook shine of it, the butchery of it, as if fasting for dear life of the one thing that will bring surcease. Well, the jug won't do me in but the Gin might, I'll start with that, yes, from tomorrow, that'll be my new trick or treat. They'll come to ferry me away yet, it'll be a gas, I won't know, I'll have stepped out of myself finally and be alone again once more, without sound. Well, I could down a bottle or two and be done with it, that might do the trick, with some luck, perhaps, and I the lucky one, indeed, the lucky one to be removed. Yet still these hands that clutch at nothing I have a certain fondness for, these eyes that sink further and further into my skull behind the furrows of lines that assault my gait like scars. What once...what once?...regret what?...regret that...rot and spectres...I laugh but I'm silent, the laughter of the talon...I do not have the indecency to laugh in company, ah they were of no use, those pedlars of love. My blood-red purchase made for better love than what they gave to me, dressed up like love's charlatan, in the name of family. No no. They were all cunts, not a word, not a kind word to say of them, I've forgotten it all, much of the time, which is the good enough, no jangle in that, too old to fuck with the dreaming sense of streaming clouds shimmering. I. Excised to the bone. It's noted, yes. Ah yes, at that jangle again, haven't you noticed? Well, I scratch my arse, I sit at my table, I make notes, noted little plagues of things, and sure who would listen to me, I'm a corrupt auld bastard, aulder than I should be, in both respects, too old to have lived and too young to feel like this. I should have thrown myself off the cliffs when I had the chance, but oh no, the ocean frightens me, I almost drowned once, as I said. A child, yes, Step back, he says, till I cast out, and me on the edge of the bank and a three feet drop into the flow. Well, I stepped back, and kept going and next thing there was nothing there and I was submerged, and my Wellington boots were filling up with water, and me sinking, sinking. And he the lug bastard that he was reefed me out of the flow with one arm and up onto the bank and me, not a bollocks notion, terrified, all said. Well out of those drenched clothes with you, he says, and me stood there shivering and naked and him feeling the hairless tiddler off of me. And then it all goes blank...And him too dead to cut the life out of with a rusty blade, the dirt-bag...Well all in all, all in all for one, or none, or not at all, no, not for one. Carnival airs are the best to take a body into some foreign purpose of extravagance. A dove lands suddenly on my windowsill before me. I raise a glass to Ms. Dove, down it, I light a smoke...

...E. still looks at me with that terrified feline gaze when I re-enter the room. I am almost surprised that she doesn't have a needle stuck in her arm or wherever else for that matter. I tell her the water's hot, to work away. She kicks off her shoes, snatches up her bag and brushes past me without uttering a sound. Well, there's still another bottle at least, time has ceased to be in this den of insanity, fuck the glass I drink it down straight, well alright, here's to it. There's not a face nor trace out there that interests me, I'll dream alone of the nothing else. Outside, the children pass dressed in their school uniforms, no they don't teach you about searing despair, do they, in any school, nor the vice grip of the snare of being. Well what does one do as one waits?, it's been said, I'll say it again, waits for what?...

...It doesn't take me long to finish the bottle of wine, perhaps a half-hour, it's hard to tell. I figure the water must be getting cold by now, and notice that E. has neglected to take my solitary towel with her to dry herself off with. I can barely stand. I manage it somehow. Moving to the bed I waver, collapse headlong onto it. I'd rather just lay there and drift but my malignant sense of duty ushers me up, to the door and sway sway swaying out into the corridor, towel in hand. I make it to the bathroom. I knock on the door. Pause. No answer. I knock again, the door opens slightly. E. lays there naked but for her knickers, her feet up on the rim of the bath. The water is tinged with pink, no not from vaginal blood, she is stoned, asleep, a syringe hangs limply from her bruised right arm. The water is pink on account of the blood from the slash-marks on her breasts and stomach and arms. In haste, I move to the bath's edge and reach down between her legs into the melding of water and blood and unplug the bath. She's not stirring, no surprise, I check her pulse. I don't know how much she has taken and I am in no condition to try and gauge, but I know that she hasn't over-dosed. Her wounds are not so deep, but as the water disappears I notice the scar-tissue that covers her body. I reach in under her back and with a certain amount of difficulty slide her from the bath to the floor and lay her down. I then notice the Stanley knife, a creature comfort no doubt, a double-edged sword in case the customers get too freakish. I run the water and clear the traces of her being down the plughole. I lock the door from the inside, fall back against the wall. I slide down the wall onto my haunches. The tears well, but I can't. I can't move either. I can't look but I can't help myself. Her wounds are still leaking thin trickles of blood, little tributaries against her ivory flesh. Her breast ebbs and flows, slowly, her ribcage stretched against her tight skin. What a fucking jangle she's landed herself in coming to me, I'm not fit for fuck all, useless, fit for the knacker's yard, and yet what?, she's here, and that's all there is to be done or undone about it. I pick myself up from the floor, snatching up the towel I throw it over the rawness of her body. I slide her up and onto my left shoulder, almost a dalliance with the empty bathtub could have mangled both of us, but I'm steady. She's not heavy, limber as a Spring twig. I unlock the bathroom door with my right hand and we are through. I'm walking up the corridor and my neighbour's door opens right on cue. A small balding man with fuzzy shoulder-length red hair and a shock of beard. He knows me. He knows better. He says nothing. I'd kicked in his door manys a time on account of the bloody racket in the middle of the night and him pissed drunk on whiskey. Anyway we make it, I slump her down slowly onto the bed, throw the covers over her. I stagger back to the bathroom and retrieve the syringe, spoon, all of that, the Stanley knife, her clothes and bag before anyone has the chance to draw conclusions and land me in a jangle. We must live through fools, not around them. E. may be a brick wall, I can't tell. I walk back into the room and toss her stuff into the corner, place the set down onto the table amongst the other debris. I stand there wavering over her. She still looks beautiful. Amorous even. Yet what of it? All I can think of are the scars and the fresh welts across her flesh. Another drink, yes, but I'm out, there's merely a trickle of whiskey left in the bottle. I'll have to step out, she'll be out for quite a while it seems. I snatch my satchel off the hook on the door and step out, I pull the door closed behind me, step out into a world that I want no part of...

...Times denounced, times when, or perhaps, no, I care not, here?, of what?, raking up the shed skin of bloody leaves, enticed, crushed now, foreign now, in spasm of lunatic, a jig danced, held by none and wanting none, in a foothold, at the length of the wind, my crumpled hands, now I and the mirth. Ah, I laugh at myself, I am longing but one, walls, walls, and me and my table, my bottles, yes I was out today, I keep my promises, all the Gin in the world and me halfway through the first of them. Five green bottles sitting on a wall, well no, I shelved out, I bought twice for half the price. And the sun, ah I am out of breath with the sun, let it be buggered, let it be hung, lest there be worship, lest there be a tongue to lick us dry, no, not I. Gin makes a man mean, they say, well let it be so, the giggle and stomp of the vine is for nancy boys, I couldn't stomach another drop. The doomed yet undefeated, the Bull Burroughs once said, they passed on, death by predilection, a circus carousel never seen nor heard of, rock salt and the stone veins, the heart staunched, the heart submerged, and mine shredded and cast to the dogs long ago -oh how I relished the tearing of my flesh before me! Yet I, and all that was have never been anything other than this, never claimed nor solicited, no, after a time, left...alone. And so I was left to the breathe of it, and where from out of where this jangle arose, I cannot tell. Ashen logic gave birth to a dissipating sun, and the world eased further and further away from out of where there was no reaching purpose. No never a lie has passed between me and the four walls, silenced I've been but for the murmurs, noted, yes, lapsing between the unseen night and the break in the tide, that hourglass knowledge. I have never known the sky, I expect it's not like that for everyone else, no matter. Still at this ripe age, living for nothing, still keeping some kind of record. E. steps in and out of me with a cold chill, and those damned days, they lasted, they have never ceased, and me at the close of one and the beginning of it, no, no hope, it was noted then, with more hunger then, the rage/ impetus of youth playing into a death hand. Cardiac/ alack. Ah, they leave you behind so heavily as if to pare away the bone, stunt the remembering, blank spaces, empty echoes and vapours, and you just some figment in the midst, half dead and wondering -*why not me?* And yet the Gin flows, jingle, jangle, all along the banks of the Royal Canal. Ah Behan, how could I forget it, and the quarry -Ship Ahoy!, (we've not left land yet y'feckin' eejit!). Down the hatch and rot to spill, claim and be done, back, some front on him, the clown. Ah, they'd almost rot you into the ground, empty bottles lined up like memories erased, you see it now, I no longer look, there's nothing there but transparency. Eye of eye and the broken jaw, the flapping tongue of spastic light. Ah the dance, some measure by which to unshadow all, easy now, what and if. I imagine. Well live one day and die of the next, a fruitless fancy, it's a long line, it leads through the redundant pulse, the rapacious night. All in all and the love lost, moving elsewhere, shaking hands, wiping it off on your trousers. Drag now naught, unto naught, yet no-one is listening to the silent speech of the age, no-one is hearing the words, they are of dead silences. No, no eyes to greet, no eyes to turn away from, no body to expire in. The queue shifts one step, might take a jangle of ten years, death bites close to the vein, sting and sudden atrophy, shadow and in-dreaming, viciously locked to the bone. Still I am death, of which there is no question, the sparks fly, no limbo is not for the living, I'll stretch yet. I'll burn out my last breath blowing absent foreign kisses to the sky. Ah, noted. Pox. Spit into the heart of the matter and rake with gilded fingers the parchment lifelessness of devoid hours. Down the hatch and the fresh feel of it, the ever numbness of it, burning as it goes, that's the ticket. I'd dig a tunnel if it could get me out, I'd...No, no use in that, dig in the heels and wait for the day, the day will come easily and with clarity, not from some special psychosis, those were the days, ah yes the bounty of it, the terror, the stretching and the tearing, as if birthing something greater than oneself, havoc and plague and the bloody flames of being ablaze, the shimmering heat arising from the flesh like vapours from a desert highway, all aboard this train leads straight for the core from out of nowhere, yet crawling, gathering momentum, feeling it coming and....Ah, enough of that. Long days now passed, driftwood I, without a current or a shine, the course not worth the price of the ticket. Left now, hold your horses, drag 'em dry, hold high the culled absence. Sweet absence of intoxication, no no course for cowardice, opening up the skull, incisor marks of night. From what dense sun does no warmth align the sight. And all the pestilence char of shrouded teeth, jangle again, noted -ah me bollocks! Sliding now, the bottle drained dry, like a corpse into a casket into an open grave into the silence into...How we laughed, I kissed his cold skin and that was him, noble no more, no not like that I hardly killed the man, a strange thing to kiss the forehead of the dying and the dead. Well now, a confessional without a priest. I'd bugger a priest viciously rather than confess this catalogue of so-called sin -sin, my piss! Ah your worship, I think you've dropped the body of Christ and up with his skirt and in like a molten poker, tearing away, tearing away...Well no...Forever night...There was a time when I believed in excavation, long dead now. Nothing in there but a horde of vipers, with no recourse, hands cold growing into the fingers, claiming the land, still not claiming the butchery of the abattoir. I will laugh too late, I'll be too late, it'll all come unexpected if I don't. Well call cards. I'll never be done...

#12-...Nothing, cold stammer, abridged...I arrive back to find E. fully dressed, sitting on the edge of the bed. Her eyes betray the fact that she is still stoned from the junk. Swollen over, beneath the bruising. She is filing her nails onto the wooden floor. Stepping inside I close the door behind me. The wounds on her arms are still raw but it appears that they have stopped bleeding. She murmurs a subtle hello, stares up at me with dead fish eyes, no sign of anything in there. I cross the room and set my satchel down onto the table, remove a bottle, uncork it, pour two glasses. It must be no later than 11 a.m. She takes the drink from me, takes a sip and places it on the floor. I down mine and pour another. I sit back down at the table, facing her. I have a surprise for you, but you'll have to wait, she says, through her freshly lit cigarette. She offers no explanation for earlier in the morning, but I'm not in the mood for explanations, either. Let's just drink, I say, we'll just drink and let the daylight slide from view. I'll need to go out to score, she says. I ask her is she coming back, she says she doesn't know. You can fuck me in a while if you like, she says, I don't mind, it means nothing to me. You don't have to pay, you've been good to me, letting me stay here and all. They call me 'The Black Dove', but they've clipped my wings, they dole me out Smack just to keep me trading out. The more stoned I am the less I feel it, they can do pretty much anything to me and I don't care, they pay high and the cut is high. I used to be at Trinity College, but I ditched that for the Smack and wound up peddling myself until they caught the hold of me on someone else's patch. Well, they beat the shit out of me, the other whores, gutter-trash junkies, no class, no fuck all. That's how they found me. I was lying by the side of the canal, one of the bitches had stuck a screw-driver into me. I was bleeding like fuck, I could have died. Maybe better that I had, look at the fucking state of me, barely twenty-one and half fucking dead on account of the amount of Smack I'm using. I shot a fifty-bag into myself in the bath, by the way, sorry about the mess, I just get these rages and then...She lifts up her glass and takes a long swallow...Shit, I don't know, I don't even know why I came here, sanctuary?, you seemed kind, most would have just walked right past me on the road like that. There were two of them, one had a blade, I wasn't quick enough with the Stanley knife, they dragged me down an alleyway and you can guess the rest -I'm sorry about the blood on your sheets, on all counts. I ask her to give me the Stanley knife, but she says no. It's your fucking funeral, then, my dear, I say. I fill our glasses with more wine. Don't you do anything but drink?, she asks. No, not much else...Why don't you just kill yourself and get it over and done with, then, she says, it seems pretty meaningless. Yes, it is, I say, but isn't everything else? The way you're going you'll be lucky if you make it another year, so who's counting? But let's not get into lifestyle choices here, you do what you have to and I'll do what I can, we'll go from there, I'm getting there, and so are you...

...Ah, I'm coughing up more blood than some poor wretch with the bronchitis. Sick bastard that I am, I like the taste of it, it tastes like life yet more of death, of time erasing itself. Ah, the Gin swallow, the rot of it, rotting for so long, yet never enough, head in the pyre of ill-dreaming, such pox and waste and the sun blinding me, I'll have to draw the blinds -ah spit! I've stopped taking the pills, no use, worse than before, culling nothing, although they went well with the booze; I never remembered anything. And so-so-so and far away, shadowy nocturne and the bile of useless emptiness. Ah, I never asked for much and found the less and less, the dripping faucet, eyes ablaze in the night staring at the judders in the skull, contract/ retrace, and the fear and the shaking limbs. Three tall glasses to settle me back to from where I wish to be. Ah the inglorious wretchedness of the damned! And how they romanticise, these fools of some other era, these fools caught in the snare of it, much like I do myself on a good day. Outside lays this pox-ridden jangle of a world, and a snout of lovelessness, all day long the shearing, the abattoir of it, what sense?, non-sense, dis-ease, I sneeze and spray myself with blood and spittle -ah shit! I'll have to. Enough of this now. No, I'm not ready yet. A wise man said that there is no point in killing oneself as we always do it too late. Try thirty fucking years too late, having learned nothing from those slaughterhouse days back then in Dublin. What with E., the jangle of it, no I hardly loved her, I hardly knew the girl, yet there was something, she just broke in upon me, scattered stars upon my walls that glowed in the dark, smeared them with blood on that most horrendous of days. She promised me, we had a pact, no not some pox of a suicide pact, but to keep on going until one of us faltered. Ah what a sweet, beautiful girl when she wasn't stoned out of her mind on Smack. They came and carried her limp body out of the place, the arms of her slashed deep, almost to the bone and the fucking blood everywhere. I had to leave that day. I gathered up my nothingness, a few notebooks, some rags, a suitcase full, we'd sat and watched those stars she had placed meticulously glow on the walls the previous night. No, I didn't fuck her, I could have, no, I'm a man of honour, I sat there blank and she dead and the blood sprayed everywhere, bloody handprints on the walls and smears of crimson meat release, unto her finality. Ironically, it was I who was having a bath, washing away a weeks dirt -well I'd been on a drunk for sometime, it happens. And no Spring sunlight in the world could have penetrated that girl's body. And now nothing having changed and me still fit to be crossed up. I can feel it, too late for the Gin, too late for the flames of it, drawing breath more slowly now, pox and be done and steering my course for what I've always sought. Too old, ah the swarm of it, the horse's head in the bed unmade, the teeth of it, a barbed-wire chasm, vileness and candy-coated, all in all, breaking now not having sent out for the chariot to carry me home. Another bottle and the scald. How did I get here, this pox of an Italian town and the noose not taking me to where? I'll take to the bed and be done with it, bring my bottles with me. I'll not move, I'll dig my heels in. They'll not find me. They'll not find the brutality of it in me, it's noted, there'll be no speeches nor accolades. Ah, guttering flame, sweet Prince of sweet fuck all. Nothing less and nothing more in the searing winds that encircle me. Death is like nothing we know, so they say, but I've drawn my -almost- final breath manys a time. Riddle me this, riddle me three blind mice and the bitch hacking off the tails of the poor bastards. Ah, I'm gone, down the hatch, feed the endless gouge of the skull's propriety. I never killed a man, perhaps I should have, to spice up the meat of conscience. I'll just lay here, pillows curled up, bottle in hand, and then another -what of it?, it's only life, it's only existence, it's only death and what of it? And for what? So much time to burn yet never enough yet the drag beneath the ocean, the bones silent and my...undoing it all. Sleep now, as under that ancient lamp, all twined together, tired out with so much listening, so much toil and play, he said*. No I never, no not but once, no I never loved, all said undone, it's noted, yes, the heave-ho of the breast, I'm watching, there's a white-house on the coast, I'll dream of that. I'll remember nothing anymore, ah with such bile I'll fade, I close the book, it's noted, it's...

...Ah spit...Blur of static mould...Extracted...Waking again to this hilarity, covered in vomit I am and not being able to feel my bloody head. It's everywhere. I'll have to get up but I can't move, I'm still pissed drunk. Two bottles of the Gin I downed to douse the flame, and nothing -if there were gods I'd blame them, for putting the fix on me, the hex, a good laugh, ha-ha, rot. Well, what now?, begin again?, I'll have to roll out of the bed onto the floor, and leave this Shroud of Turin behind me. And me still dressed and hey-ho, it appears I've also lost control of my bowels. Can I not be killed? Am I to take the same route as E.? The veins torn out of me with my teeth?...Ah, forget about her, thirty years on and still rolling her around on my tongue like a tumour. A bath then, your Lord your worship. If I could move I'd laugh but no, between the puke and the shit -for fuck's sake how could I do anything else? I'll just lay here, I'll not move, no not even for the Divine Intervention, not for the ring-leader, not for any bastard, I'll just lay here, yes, it's noted, I might piss myself, I might die yet. Well it would have to be a sunny day outside to compound things, I'll...Well for a few hours there I was gone and a slice of death did me no harm, all said all done. I passed out again. Two baths. The first to wash away the shite and the vomit, the second to cleanse me. No I don't have a fucking rubber ducky. I sat there in the bath drinking Gin and smoking, hacking up my lungs, tra-la-la. Back at it again. At my table, notebook out, the Gin flowing, smoke furling upward like a trail of gestures forever lost. And me being the sum and summation of all things and the light of day that I am can find nothing -no, there's a surprise yet, nowhere else to be. Ah this Italian temperament makes me ill at heart, but no, never to set foot on Irish soil again, I'd rather garrotte myself, set myself on fire and burn all the way through as I walked the streets. Yet still you can't walk the streets of Italy drunk without being regarded as being something of the plague. Pox and rattle, feckin' Espresso and Gelatino -what kind of a fucking existence is that? I suppose you could venture that being a half-dead drunk intent upon self-consumption isn't much of a life either but I don't care, I still have my standards. I'll rage and I'll cuss any bastard that gets in the way of me, and no pox bastard will ever change that. Nothing like a rut to keep you on the right path, a wise man once said. Ah they're all burning up inside of me, mercury blood ablaze, skull and tongue, all of the rest of them burned out, and me the last of them. Ah the dance, I'll dance the jig of this Danse Macabre, I'll burrow through the echoes, I'll remember if it has ceased to be, if it kills me in the process. No, I never wanted anything, and I found less, I've said it before. So much I'll never tell, I just sit here and fill myself, I'll note, no I'll never leave this place of echoes and vapours, poxes and riddles, I'll live just to spite the butchery of it, I'll devour the essence and spit shit at the hyenas. And from out of this pall-bearer's nothing nothing else will arise, as from you, nothing else will arise. And that will be my sun, the un-dead sky of rigid bones, there, sunlight spilling into my room with a view, this nowhere, this dreaming of...I never did. I never will...Ah the sudden...Noted,

noted, it's noted...Better cleft than dead...Or...Sweet avalanche of endless   waste,   its   traces   sublime...